Also By R.W. Wallace

The Ghost Detective Series
Beyond the Grave
Unveiling the Past
Beneath the Surface

Ghost Detective Short Stories
Just Desserts
Lost Friends
Family Bonds
Common Ground
Till Death
Family History
Heritage
Eternal Bond
New Beginnings
Severed Ties

Short Story Collections
Deep Dark Secrets
A Thief in the Night

R.W. WALLACE
Author of the Ghost Detective Series

TALES
FROM THE
TRENCHES

A YOUNG ADULT SHORT STORY
COLLECTION

Tales From the Trenches

by R.W. Wallace

"First Impressions" Copyright © 2021 by R.W. Wallace

"Unexpected Consequences" Copyright © 2021 by R.W. Wallace

"The Lucia Crown" Copyright © 2021 by R.W. Wallace

"Let Them Eat Cake" Copyright © 2021 by R.W. Wallace

"The Art of Pretending" Copyright © 2021 by R.W. Wallace

Cover by the author

Cover Illustration 85978840 © Sandra Matic | 123rf.com

All characters and events in this book, other than those clearly in the public domain, are fictitious and any resemblance to real persons, living or dead, is purely coincidental.

All rights reserved. No part of this publication may be reproduced, distributed, or transmitted in any form or by any means, including photocopying, recording, or other electronic or mechanical methods, without the prior written permission of the publisher, except in the case of brief quotations embodied in critical reviews and certain other noncommercial uses permitted by copyright law.

www.rwwallace.com

ISBN: [979-10-95707-77-6]

First Edition

TABLE OF CONTENTS

Introduction	1
First Impressions	3
Unexpected Consequences	29
The Lucia Crown	55
Let Them Eat Cake	77
The Art of Pretending	99
Author's Note	124
About the Author	125
Also by R.W. Wallace	126

INTRODUCTION

As I've been putting my short stories into collections, I've been searching for common elements, so that I can logically group certain stories together. Sometimes this means genre, sometimes theme.

For this one, I originally aimed for a Young Adult audience. The majority of my stories are aimed at an adult audience, so I didn't have a million stories to choose from here and I wondered if I would be able to find a common red thread.

As I started sifting through the stories, I discovered there *was* a theme.

Apparently, when I write high school age characters, I write about bullying. You'd think I was bullied in my youth or something.

Oh wait, I was. Which, yeah, probably explains things.

Anyways, what doesn't break you makes you stronger, right? That is what they say? I guess I have to agree.

As would the characters of the stories of this volume. The stories are of varying genres — we have two mysteries, one science fiction, one fantasy, and one holiday story, some with romance elements, some without, some featuring LGBT+ characters, some going the more classic route — so I hope there will be a little something for everyone.

One thing is certain: I had a lot of fun writing these stories, and I'm thrilled to be able to share them with you!

R.W. Wallace
www.rwwallace.com

FIRST IMPRESSIONS

Being the new girl in school is never fun.

I'm used to it, though. Spotting potential new friends, identifying the cliques to avoid, figuring out the school's layout... Been there, done that.

Being accused of murder before the first class even starts? That's new.

ONE

Everybody knows it's no fun to be the new kid in school. It's important to get off to a good start, make a good first impression.

My first day as a senior in my new school? I got accused of murder.

So much for first impressions.

ೞ

I prepared for this day for weeks.

I studied the maps, both of the town and the school. How long would it take me to walk to school? Ten minutes. Was there a bus I could take if it rained? No, better get a decent raincoat and an umbrella. Where was the nearest supermarket, gas station, or anything else that could keep me supplied in sugar in case of emergency? There was a tiny supermarket not even a hundred meters from the school, and a gas station a little further out for when the supermarket was closed.

The school itself seemed boringly predictable (total fail in the research department on this point, the school was anything but). The yard was a square, surrounded by awnings on all sides. Two buildings stood two stories tall, one on the east side of the yard, the other on the west. It was one of those constructs from the seventies, one huge, beige brick, with hundreds of identical windows, managing to look like a prison even without the bars (actually, now that I think of it, there were bars—on the ground floor windows). To the north, the school was shut off from the rest of the world by a ten-meter-high wall (adding to the prison feels), and to the south, a simple fence with a gate that was guarded by a lady who seemed like she'd been seated there since the seventies.

Three days before school started, my mom took me shopping. It's an activity I usually loathe, but I needed to look presentable (but preferably with ripped holes in the right places), cool (but not too cool, I'm a nice girl and a bit of a nerd at heart), and approachable (because there was no way I'd be the one to approach the others).

Less than two hours, a few euros (in my mom's case) and several tears (in my case) later, I arrived home ready to start a new and better life.

Little did I know that having the right rips in my jeans would soon be the least of my worries.

TWO

THE SCHOOL OPENED its doors (well, the door in the fence, not the doors to the buildings, as I was soon to discover) at eight. Classes started at eight thirty.

Being a good girl, and terrified of being late, I went through the gate at two past eight.

You'd expect the school yard to be empty at that ungodly hour, but no. Seemed like my future classmates (whichever ones they were—this school had five hundred students and only twenty-five of them were in my class) were eager to come back to school—or at the very least, to meet up with their friends that they hadn't seen in over two months.

I sidled along the west building, keeping to the shadows offered by the awning, while trying to keep an eye on everyone in the schoolyard.

My first mistake.

Since I was so focused on every single movement I could

see in the center of the yard, I didn't look at where I was putting my feet. So when I stepped straight onto some poor soul's ankle, I didn't even have the reflex to not put all my weight down, or side-step, or *something*. Anything. No, I just continued walking, putting all my weight on my foot before tripping a little because, well, someone's ankle isn't all that stable.

I heard a loud yelp, followed by an *oof*—as I landed ass-first in the lap of my poor target.

Broke my fall quite nicely, so I bounced right back up.

Him, not so much.

"I'm so sorry!" I yelled, putting my hands on my cheeks, then reaching toward his ankle (as if that would do any good at this point), back to my face, toward his stomach (where he probably had an ass-shaped imprint).

I ended up shoving my hands in my pockets.

"I'm so sorry," I repeated. "I didn't see you there."

The poor guy curled into a fetal position, with one hand on his stomach and the other on his ankle. I hadn't gotten a good look at his face, but he seemed tall (then again, everyone's tall compared to me) and had short, curly hair. His skin a smooth brown a couple of shades darker than what I could obtain by spending three months in the sun. Jeans ripped at the knees, and his t-shirt a plain white affair that might have hugged his muscles if he'd had any to write home about.

"How is that even possible?" he wheezed.

"Should've paid attention, man," a voice called from behind me. "She was walking like a blind woman."

I turned to look at the voice's origin and was surprised to

discover that the entire wall was occupied by guys, propped up against the dirty wall, their long legs spread out in front of them.

How had I walked past all of them and not noticed a single one? How had I avoided stepping on *them*?

The guy who spoke must have read the question on my face. "We all pulled our legs out of the way," he explained. "Gotta watch where you're going, man."

I briefly considered informing him I wasn't a man, but quickly figured it wasn't worth the effort.

I bent down and patted the air above the wounded guy's head, saying, "I'm really, really sorry. Won't happen again, I promise." Then I took off.

Well, that was one guy that wouldn't be asking me out anytime soon.

At the far end of the building, I found an unoccupied section of wall and decided this was my spot. This was where I would observe the cliques of this school and figure out which one I wanted to be a part of.

Managing to actually integrate said group would be step two, and I'd worry about that once step one was completed.

I quickly concluded that the group of blonde girls standing only a few meters away were not my type. For one, I don't have blonde hair, and that seemed to be a requirement. In fact, three of the girls were nagging the fourth one because she'd let her roots grow out over the summer. No amount of arguing that she'd done it on purpose and that it was the latest thing in Paris could persuade the trio. In less than five minutes, the tune of the fourth one changed to, "I just haven't had the time, but I'll get it done tonight."

I inwardly rolled my eyes. These were the cool girls, I just knew it. They're the same everywhere (okay, they don't all have blonde hair, but you get my drift) and anyone's best policy should be to stay as far away as possible. Even the girls *inside* these groups aren't safe. They're like cannibals, frequently eating their own, to make sure everybody stays on their toes, and to confirm the position of whoever the leader is.

I'm pretty sure girls like these are the actual reason other girls never go alone to the bathroom. Everybody makes fun of girls always going in pairs, but they don't realize it's a survival thing. You do *not* want to find yourself alone in a room with the four Blondies.

And now I needed to use the toilet.

I checked my watch. It was only ten past eight.

I looked around, searching for a door with a woman on it. Or even a man. I'm not that picky when I'm desperate.

Since I was increasingly convinced that I wouldn't be able to find a bathroom until the school officially opened in twenty minutes, I was getting desperate real fast.

There had to be some place we could use the restroom while we were out during recess, right?

I pushed my way past the Blondie group and approached a short red-head. I had yet to see a red-head as the leader in a school, so I figured she was a safe bet.

"Excuse me," I said, flashing her my best smile. "You wouldn't happen to know where the restrooms are? I'm new in this school."

The girl looked at me with slightly unfocused brown eyes and for a moment I worried she was a foreign exchange student who didn't speak the language.

She squinted down at me, then her eyebrows shot up. "Oh, sorry, I thought you were Léna." She pointed to the other building, at the northernmost corner. "The toilets are over there."

"Thank you." Hefting my backpack higher on my back, I almost sprinted across the yard, all the while searching with my eyes for one of those wonderful signs.

I found it exactly where the girl told me I would, but a group of at least fifteen girls were blocking my way.

"Excuse me," I tried as I pushed my way into the throng. "I need to use the restroom, please."

"Door's locked," a dark-eyed beauty told me when I tried to get past her.

I was getting really desperate, and even though I realized she was probably right, I needed to check for myself.

Needless to say, that group of girls would not be my friends, either. Stabbing someone with your elbow as you try to get past them, or stepping on someone's sandaled feet, are not the best first impressions if you want to make friends.

To make matters worse, the door was indeed locked.

I checked my watch again. Eight thirteen.

I wasn't going to make it.

So like I always do in stressful situations, I improvised.

And no, this is never a good idea, but I never learn.

I noticed there was a very narrow space between the building and the huge north wall cutting us off from the rest of the world. When I went to check, I saw that there were windows, most certainly leading to the bathrooms. It was one of those wide openings that are almost at the ceiling—so you get light in, but nobody can stand outside and perv on the people taking care of business on the inside.

I jumped up to look—the window was cracked open.

Okay, that did it. I was going in.

I abandoned my backpack in the corner, wrongfully thinking I'd be back to get it in a minute or two. Then I took aim, crouched down, and jumped.

Not at the window, mind. It was just too high. I jumped at the wall. Then used that as a jumping board to bound back at the school building.

I knocked my forehead into concrete, but I managed to grab hold of the windowsill and pull myself up.

Using an elbow to force the window open, I poured myself through the opening, and jumped into the bathroom feet first.

Victory!

A quick glance told me there was no way I was going out the way I came in because it was higher up the wall in here, and I had nothing to use for purchase. Right then I didn't care.

I just wanted to pee.

Which was to become my main line of defense.

I ran to the closest stall, slammed open the door, and started opening my jeans before I was even inside. It wasn't like anybody else was going to come in there, right?

As I could *finally* let free, my teeth had goosebumps and I uttered a shivering moan.

At which point, a voice said, "What on Earth is going on in here? Do *not* tell me someone's started in on the depravities *before* the school year has even started."

That was definitely an adult.

And that ray of light coming in from the left? Yup, probably from the open door.

Never one to abort any action once I've started, I stayed seated.

A woman stepped in front of my open stall. She was tall, blonde, carrying an extra kilo or two around the midsection, and dressed like a hippie. Long flowery skirt, loose white blouse. I guessed her hair was naturally straight because the lack of free curls definitely looked odd.

"*What* is going on here?" Only teachers could put that much accusation into a simple question.

"What does it look like?" I replied. I was finally done but didn't want to get up in front of the teacher, so I stayed seated.

Her eyes scanned the room as she gesticulated with her skinny arms. "It looks like—" She drew in a quick breath.

Screamed.

Some sort of survival instinct kicked in for me, and I slammed both arms outward, holding on to the walls of my stall. Maybe I was expecting them to fall down on me?

I did *not* think of getting dressed.

So naturally, when the group of girls from earlier swarmed the restroom, I was still sitting on the toilet with my jeans around my ankles.

When the titters started, I decided it was time to cut my losses. Jumped up and pulled at my jeans at lightning speed. Of course, the panties didn't quite follow, so they sat halfway down my ass, making it feel like I was still naked.

The teacher was still screaming.

"Hey," the pretty girl from earlier said as she looked into the stall next to mine. "Who killed Madame Couteloup?"

THREE

So there I was, sitting in the headmaster's office with two police officers staring at me from across the headmaster's desk. The man himself was leaning against the window (with bars, since we were on the ground floor), but hadn't said a word since I walked through the door. Next to him stood the hippie teacher from earlier, who *finally* stopped screaming the minute she saw the uniforms.

I wondered if I got two female officers because they believed I was most likely to confess to women, or if there really were a lot of women in the police force today. I considered looking into it as a potential career.

"Did you kill Madame Couteloup?" the youngest of the two asked me. She had silky black hair and makeup so subtle you couldn't even tell it was there unless you looked for it. I was thinking being a cop couldn't be that bad if she could look this good on the job. Then the question sank in.

Maybe make sure I wasn't convicted of murder before deciding to become a cop.

"Of course I didn't!" I said. Maybe I should call my lawyer. Or my mom. That's what they always did in the American series on TV. Called their lawyers, that is. I wasn't even sure that was how it worked in France.

Should've watched more French sitcoms.

Do French police procedurals even exist? There was so much crap on TV, I seriously considered giving up on it altogether until my parents got Netflix. Since then I'd become *slightly* addicted.

"Mademoiselle Gérard," the old police officer said (she must have been at least forty, possibly even older given the number of gray hairs I spotted). "You were discovered on the scene of the crime, not having raised the alarm yourself, and with your pants down."

I frowned at her. "You make me sound like a sexual offender. You don't get caught with your pants down in a murder case." What *do* you get caught with? A smoking gun?

"And yet," the old one said, "you were."

"I needed to pee!" I explained. "The door was locked, so I went through the window. I never looked inside the stall where Madame what's-her-name was found. If I had, I assure you, I would have raised the alarm."

Possibly after relieving myself, but I didn't say that out loud.

The old one narrowed her eyes slightly and bent her head to write something in a black notebook I hadn't noticed until now.

I craned my neck trying to see what she was writing, but the angle was all wrong.

"What makes you say the door was locked?"

"I…I checked the door," I said. "It didn't open. And the other girls told me it was closed."

The old one continued taking notes while the young one talked. "Which girls?"

"Uh…" I looked to the headmaster for help, but he stood there like a statue, making me wonder if he was even awake. "I'm new in this school," I explained. "I don't know anybody."

"So a girl you don't know tells you the door's locked and you automatically believe her?"

"Why would she lie?" I caught myself before answering that question myself. "And I checked. It was locked."

"Actually," the young one said, "It wasn't. The hinges are a little rusty, so you have to push quite hard for it to open."

I was floored. Though not really surprised. It's always the same, isn't it? Step on others to get higher. Take no prisoners.

Those girls had taken one look at me and decided it was more fun to tell me the bathroom was closed than to let me through and explain how to get the door open.

"I didn't know that," I said, my voice small and uneven. I decided I didn't need to look the officers in the eyes and studied the edge of the headmaster's desk instead.

It was made of wood.

That was all I got.

"We asked the other students about you," one of the officers said. I couldn't tell them apart just from their voices. "Seems like you have a tendency toward violence."

"What?" My gaze snapped up. "Nobody here even knows my name!"

"And yet you've managed to assault several of them already."

I stared at the two women in incomprehension. I turned to the headmaster and the hippie teacher, but they were no better. Serious expressions all around, and accusation obvious in their eyes.

Four adults in the room, and they all believed I killed some teacher I'd never even met!

"One boy," the young one said, "claims you stepped and sat on him while he was listening to music, minding his own business."

"I didn't see—," I started, but nobody was listening.

"Another girl claims you pretended to be her friend Léna in order to extract information from her."

"I asked her where the bathroom—"

"Five different girls claim you attacked them with your elbows and stepped on their toes as you, for some reason, had to go *through* their group."

"I had to *pee*, and they were blocking the door to the bathroom!"

I finally got to finish a sentence, but my yelling was followed by a resounding silence.

The old one filled an entire little page with notes, and as she turned the page, she asked, "How well did you know Madame Couteloup?"

"I didn't." I drew a deep breath and let it out slowly. "I want to call my mom."

The headmaster spoke up for the first time, making me jump in my chair. "She's already been notified of the situation. She's on her way."

That didn't sound as reassuring as it should.

The young one folded her hands and cocked her head as she narrowed her eyes at me. "What did Madame Couteloup do to deserve your wrath, young lady?"

"I didn't even know her! The only time I ever saw her she was already dead."

Nobody believed me, of course. And although I didn't know the dead teacher before, during the upcoming interrogation, I started to get a pretty good picture.

The old one: "Did she put you in a class with people you didn't like?"

"I wouldn't know. I don't know which class I'm in yet, and I don't know anybody in this school."

The new one: "Did you make sexual advances on her and she turned you down?"

What?

The old one: "Did *she* make advances on *you*?"

Ew.

The headmaster (I must not be the only one thinking this interrogation was going off the rails): "Did she accuse you of something you didn't do? Didn't give you a chance to explain? Went straight for the punishments?"

With the theme of the previous questions, a frisson ran through me at the mention of punishments, but I was going to assume he was talking about detention or extra homework. I shook my head.

The hippie teacher: "Did she give you a lecture on how the world would go under if we all wanted to eat ecological food? Did she tell you that you were egoistical and judgmental?"

I shook my head.

The headmaster: "Maybe she refused your request to use the bathroom, claiming it wouldn't open until eight thirty, only to use the premises herself?"

I was less and less offended by their questions, and more and more convinced the dead woman was one of those teachers you avoid at all costs. The kind adults talk about thirty years later to illustrate how awful school was back in their time.

The police officers seemed happy to let the teacher and headmaster do the interrogation. In fact, the old one was still taking notes, and the young one had shifted in her chair so she had both me and the school employees in her sight.

The hippie teacher: "Did she steal your snack, claiming she did you a service since it didn't have an ecological label?"

The hippie teacher: "Did she brag about her vacation on Isle de Ré, going on and on about the hunks who supposedly flirted with her on the beach?"

The surreal direction this interrogation was going in made my fear and stress fall away. I forgot I was accused of murder.

"I've been to Isle de Ré," I told her. "If you like some calm when you go to the beach, it's not ideal, honestly. And the people are…fake."

"Exactly!" the hippie teacher exclaimed, waving her arms. "It's for fake people who have no real friends and just want to show off their tan and their money."

I nodded. "Then why do you care that she taunts you about it? If it's not actually something you want?"

I might have been the youngest person in the room, but I felt like I just might have been the only one with the right life experience to get through to this woman. I'd changed schools so many times over the past ten years, I'd literally stopped counting. My dad could never keep a job for more than a year (his record being a month and a half) and every time he changed jobs, we had to change cities.

I didn't know what it was that he did which made a move a necessity, and I didn't want to know.

What I did know was that the new girl was rarely welcomed with open arms.

I'd decided it was mostly due to fear and jealousy. Fear that I might take their place, or somehow modify the power structure that was already in place. Jealousy because I was awesome.

Yes, that was what I was going with. Deal with it.

If you looked at it that way, the verbal aggressions from fellow students weren't that bad. They criticized my clothes? Probably meant they were dope. They claimed I wasn't cool enough? It was obvious to them that I was capable of taking their place if I wanted. They purposely didn't invite me to parties when the entire school was going? Their loss. I'd just hang out with my real friends.

Because no matter which school, no matter which city, every school had nice people. You just needed to find them.

"I'm sure there are other teachers in this school," I told the hippie teacher. "People who are nice. The mean ones are just noise, you know."

"That's easy for you to say!" the teacher said, her eyes going a little too wide for comfort. "You haven't suffered the woman for ten long years."

I pitied the woman, I really did.

School can be a mean place. But the thing that saves us is that it's not forever. Junior high is just four years. High school just three. Now, a year can seem interminable when you're suffering, but if you do manage to put things into perspective, it's possible to just hunker down and power through.

But this woman, the hippie teacher, was stuck here. She'd chosen school as her place of work, and so had her bully.

"She was really that mean, huh?" I wanted to go over and give the woman a hug, but something told me to stay put.

I was vaguely aware of the three other people in the room—I heard the headmaster's raspy breath and the old one's pencil scratching across the notepad—but all my focus was on the bully victim.

"What did she do this time?" I asked.

The teacher's breath came in irregular gasps and a single tear streaked down her cheek. Her hands curled into fists at her sides. "She had a picture," she said, her voice wobbly.

"A picture of what?" Not that I really needed to know, I saw where this was going.

"Of me working in my back yard. She must have been visiting with one of my neighbors." Her eyes were distant, probably looking back to the time it happened. "It was really hot and humid, and I had a thousand weeds to get rid of. So I decided to work wearing just an old bikini.

"In the picture, you can see the top of my ass, the cellulite on my thighs, and my stomach bunching into a…huge, fat blob." She met my eyes, imploring me to understand. "She was going to leave them around school, so all the kids would find them."

Being bullied by a fellow teacher was one thing. If she also had to suffer the taunts of her students, probably for years to come, I could understand her desperation. Even I might have found that to be too much.

Kids can be *mean*.

"Killing her wasn't the right solution, though," I told her.

She hung her head, her straight hair falling forward to cover her face. "I know," she whispered. "But she had the pictures in her purse, ready to distribute, and I *panicked*."

Holding my breath, I turned to meet the old lady police officer's eyes. Did that really just happen?

She nodded at me and mouthed, *good job*.

There was some relief at no longer being suspected of murder, but mostly I felt sad. A woman who'd been bullied for years finally had enough and wanted to stand up for herself, only to end up even worse off.

The headmaster straightened. "I believe you may return to class," he said.

Nodding, I stood up. I took a step toward the door, then changed my mind.

I ran to the hippie teacher and embraced her in a hug.

FOUR

"Come sit over here." The pretty girl from in front of the bathroom that morning waved me over to her seat by the window as I made my way toward the back of the class. "Saved you a spot."

Word had spread about one teacher offing the other, and rumor had it I knew all the juicy details. The Blondies tried to befriend me over lunch (it seemed like they'd even be ready to forego the hair color rule for me), and now this group.

"Thanks," I said, "but I've always preferred the dark side of the room." I point in that direction, only to be met with a pair of dark, sparkly eyes.

Pretty.

Why was he looking at me like that?

I slowly made my way toward him—couldn't really go anywhere else after what I said to the pretty girl—trying to figure out if I was supposed to know him from somewhere.

"There's a free spot here," he said, waving to the chair next to him. He had his foot propped up on it, which might explain why the seat was still free. The seats at the back of a classroom were always the first to be filled.

He lowered his foot to the ground, rather gingerly for a seventeen-year-old.

Then I really noticed his clothes. Ripped jeans. White t-shirt. Brown skin and curly black hair.

"You're the guy I stepped on this morning!" I exclaimed. I felt my cheeks growing warm and seriously considered sitting next to the pretty girl.

He flashed a smile at me, and I went a little weak in the knees. Who cares if he didn't fill out his t-shirt. This guy had *charm*.

"You may have to make it up to me," he said. "I wouldn't mind a little help with Maths." He nodded to the blackboard where the maths teacher had yet to make an appearance.

He pulled out the chair for me, never taking his eyes off mine. "And maybe a coffee or an ice cream after school?"

I dropped into the chair, my backpack still on my back. "Sure," I managed to say.

Turns out you *can* remedy a first impression. Who knew?

UNEXPECTED CONSEQUENCES

Greg has had it with his parents fighting. He's had enough of being blamed and criticized for everything.

Greg wants a new life. Preferably one without his father.

And the bubbles in Grenoble promise just that.

THE CITY OF Grenoble slumbered under a blanket of mist. High up, above the mountainous Alps surrounding the city, the sky still appeared to be blue. Maybe. It was a bit like lying in bed at night waiting for your parents to stop fighting; you knew they'd tire eventually, and that morning would come and everyone would be okay, but in the present moment it was hard to believe.

Greg had never felt such oppressive heat before. His lungs protested the arrival of the moist air and did their best to get it back out as soon as possible. His body was covered in a sheen of sweat and his entire back was soaked through because of his backpack. He was pretty sure drops of sweat dripped to the ground behind him.

How did the citizens of Grenoble live in this climate, day in and day out? As Greg trudged down the sidewalk of the endless Cours Jean Jaures, he studied the people around him.

For the most part, they seemed to ignore the fact that they

were melting away, a drop of sweat at the time. The women wore summer dresses, some skimpy, some more adapted for office wear. The men sported t-shirts or short-sleeved button-downs, mostly in fabrics that didn't darken too much when soaked in sweat.

Almost everybody glanced regularly at the sky, and many turned their heads in direction of the city center as if to check for something.

Greg didn't see anything other than large, dark stone buildings lining the avenue he'd chosen, and a blurry, small mountaintop emerging straight ahead—probably the Bastille, his reason for coming here in the first place.

He'd been walking for three days straight. He'd left Lyon Saturday night, and now here he was in Grenoble, a hundred kilometers later, with aching legs, blisters on his feet, and a sunburned nose.

But he was free, and he'd never felt better.

Still, a pause wouldn't be a bad idea.

Greg pulled his worn wallet out of his back pocket—damp with sweat, how nice—to check on his finances. He'd brought all his savings, which amounted to about one hundred and fifty euros, plus two twenties he'd lifted from his dad's jacket on his way out the door.

Just thinking about it gave him the hives, but he told himself—like he had hundreds of times since leaving home—that he'd never have to worry about his dad again. If he got mad, it wasn't Greg's problem.

It might become his mom's problem, but hey, she knew how to stand up for herself.

He had eighty euros left. Not much to live on, but he wasn't supposed to need to live here for more than a day or two more. He could certainly afford something to drink, especially since he was feeling a little light-headed and wasn't certain he'd make it to the Bastille without some sustenance.

Spotting several red parasols and grey, metallic chairs, Greg advanced down one of the narrow, cobbled streets running perpendicular to the wide Cours Jean Jaures. The café was named le voyageur tranquille, which Greg found to be fitting. At least that was the goal.

He ordered a diabolo menthe, lemonade with mint syrup, and a ham sandwich. He eased into one of the chairs so he'd be facing the small square with its cutesy fountain and let out a contented sigh. Unable to resist, he lifted his feet to the chair opposite.

"Long day, huh?" The female voice came from Greg's left.

A girl, probably about Greg's age, with long, curly brown hair, large brown eyes, and cheeks so chubby they made Greg think of a hamster, sat at the next table with a milkshake in front of her.

"Uh huh," Greg replied and turned away from her.

"Except it's only nine in the morning," she continued, clearly oblivious to the fact that Greg just wanted to be left alone. "How'd you manage to get so tired already? Do you not practice enough sports? It's really important, you know, to stay in shape. Even at fifteen."

Greg snapped his gaze back to the girl. How did she know his age?

"You look like you're in shape," the girl continued as she appraised him from head to foot. "Not too fat, not too skinny." She leaned down to get a good look at his legs. "With calves like that, I'd say you're a football player. My brother has the same ones. No? Running track maybe? You look familiar, by the way. Should I know you from somewhere?"

Greg didn't know what to make of the girl. She was so… alive. And exuberant. Nothing like what he was used to at home. He didn't know how he was supposed to react.

The girl either didn't notice Greg's doubts or didn't care. "I'm Amélie, by the way," she prattled on. "I live just down the street. I usually come here for breakfast when I don't have to be at school until ten. I just love watching people walk by, wondering what they do for a living, who their friends are, where they're going. Don't you find that stuff fascinating?"

Greg continued staring, his mouth now hanging open.

She must have read something in his expression. "Oh, I'm not judging you for the whole sports thing, you know. It might not be obvious, with my cheeks taking up three quarters of my face and all, but I do lots of sports. I play volleyball, and I'm part of a circus group. I specialize in walking on a giant ball—it's just so much fun. Have you ever tried it?"

Greg managed a shake of his head.

A sandwich and the green glass of diabolo menthe appeared on the table in front of Greg. "That'll be seven euros, please," the waiter said.

Shaking himself back into the present, Greg pulled out a ten and waited for the waiter to give him his change.

The minute the man disappeared back inside the café, Amélie started talking again.

"Do you mind if I come join you?" she asked. "It'll keep you from getting a crick in your neck from turning like that."

Without waiting for Greg to reply, she left her seat, and brought her milkshake to Greg's table.

"I won't be able to people-watch as well from here," she said. "With my back to the square and all. But at least I can watch you. You seem interesting."

Greg had been ready to tell her to go back to her table, but her last comment changed his mind. She found him interesting? Nobody had ever told him that before. He'd always just been boring Greg, who never said anything in class or during football practice, and who was never allowed to go anywhere.

Deciding she probably wouldn't mind if he just stayed silent, he grabbed his sandwich and took a bite.

His eyes closed in bliss. He'd been hungrier that he'd realized. He'd had a decent meal last night, in some small village in the pass where roads and trains snaked into the basin occupied by Grenoble, but since then he'd walked through the night, allowing only two short stops for rest.

"You didn't get out of bed an hour ago," Amélie said.

Greg opened his eyes to meet hers but didn't stop chewing. He took another bite, figuring that would be a good excuse not to answer her statement.

"You look way too tired to have just gotten out of bed," Amélie insisted. The playful gleam in her eye from earlier was replaced by something more assessing. "I can smell you from here, you've been sweating in that t-shirt for way too long, and your legs can't seem to stop trembling."

Greg lowered his legs from the chair to the ground, but that didn't stop his muscles from spasming.

"Did you walk here?" Amélie's eyes were boring into Greg's now, her gaze amazingly intense for someone with such a cute and round face.

Greg took a sip of his drink. The coolness of the ice cubes and the sharp sting of the mint felt wonderful, but unfortunately, didn't help with changing the subject. Greg tried just keeping his mouth shut and finish his drink, but for some reason, Amélie didn't jump in to fill the silence.

When Greg reluctantly put his empty glass back on the table and took another bite of his sandwich, Amélie nodded as if to herself.

"You're here to pass over, aren't you?"

Greg's legs stilled under the table. His heart thumped a beat like his father practicing on his boxing ball, and his hands shook as they lowered to his lap, his sandwich finished.

"Don't worry," Amélie said, her voice soft and kind. "Nobody's judging you. But that's it, right?"

Greg gulped and nodded.

A moment of silence, then Amélie clapped her hands as if she were a teacher calling a class of ten-year-olds to order. "All right, then. I guess I'll have to help."

Greg straightened and his eyes shot to meet hers. "I don't need your help."

"Easy," Amélie said, her hands going up in surrender. "I

didn't say you needed it. Eh…all right, I did say I have to help, didn't I. Yeah, that's not what I meant. I mean I'd love to help. I'm good at helping with this stuff."

"This stuff?"

"Passing over." Amélie's dark eyes suddenly seemed out of place in her face, as if she'd swapped them with an old lady's.

They stared at each other for what felt like an eternity. The waiter came to collect their empty glasses, the couple at the table next to them finished their coffees and left, and an old man settled in at their place to read his paper.

"Do you know what you want?" Amélie asked finally.

Greg's eyebrows drew together in a frown. "What I want?"

"Where do you want to pass over to?"

"There's…" Greg hated opening himself up to ridicule like this, but Amélie seemed like a really nice girl. He still had to force the words out. "There's more than one place I could go?"

"Place and place." Amélie tipped her head from one side to the other as she seemed to try on the taste of her words before letting them out of her mouth. "It's all the same place, really. You won't come out on the other side and find a beach resort or anything."

"But they say it's a different place."

"They do say that." Amélie's hand rubbed up and down her thigh. "But it's not the locale that's important. It's the people, the feelings, the actions. Those can be different."

Greg stared at her as his frustration rose in his chest. "I don't understand," he finally ground out through clenched teeth.

Amélie broke into a brilliant smile, her pensive expression dismissed in a second. "No worries! I'll explain it to you as we go."

"As we go?"

"Sure." She got up and grabbed Greg's hand, effectively dragging him out of his chair and after her across the square. Greg just barely managed to snatch his backpack along before it was left behind.

"They're all down in the city center," Amélie explained. "It's very rare for a bubble to appear at more than five hundred meters from the foot of the Bastille."

"A bubble?" Greg was so busy trying to keep up, both physically as she basically ran down the street, and mentally as she talked about things he'd never heard of before, that he wasn't even worried about looking stupid.

Amélie slowed down to allow Greg to catch up. "A bubble is what we call the portals that allow people to pass through to other worlds. They're in the shape of a sphere, and when they arrive, they always float down from the sky like God is up there having fun blowing bubbles."

They were back on the large avenue that Greg had walked down earlier, and it was even busier than before. Cars were crawling along at pedestrian speed in all four lanes, and the people walking to work or school advanced at a brisk pace, making Greg suspect that they were all running late for something or other.

Amélie weaved her way down the sidewalk, pulling Greg by the elbow, either because she was afraid he wouldn't be able to avoid a collision on his own, or to make sure he didn't make a run for it.

"Each bubble has its own…characteristics," Amélie explained. "You can make one type of request from it, not just anything." She met Greg's gaze. "Do you understand this? It's really important."

Greg shook his head.

She pulled on Greg's elbow again as she increased their speed. "There's this one bubble that's really popular, where you can get one person to change his views of you. Like, if your wife doesn't love you anymore, you can go to a world where she actually still does. Real popular with couples on the verge of divorce, obviously, but also with people who are convinced their parents don't love them."

She went silent as her gaze turned distant. "I've always wondered what happened with those people. I mean, logically, don't all parents love their kids? Maybe they just didn't know how to show it, or that they needed to show it better. So what happens when you ask the bubble to change how a person feels about you when that person is already feeling that thing?"

Greg had never felt more lost in a conversation, and had no answer to her question, but his mind was reeling with the possibilities.

Maybe he could go to a world where his parents loved him?

Except it seemed like you could only request the change in one person, so he'd have to choose between his mom and his dad. And he suspected that Amélie's theory was right; that his parents did love him, in their own way. It just wasn't a way that Greg could live with any longer.

"There's another one, right in the middle of Place Grenette," Amélie continued when it became clear that Greg had nothing to add to this conversation. "It's the biggest bubble I've ever seen—and I've made sure to see all the known ones—and it gives me the hives. You can ask for a person to not exist. Not for the person to die, but to never have existed."

Greg stopped in his tracks.

A world without his dad. How would his mom behave if his dad wasn't there to influence her, to make her want to change for him?

Amélie had walked on without Greg, but now she came storming back.

"Oh, no you don't!" she hissed in his face, an angry blush covering her cheeks. "You do not want to go there. Think about the consequences!" With a glance at the sky, she grabbed Greg's hand and pulled him with her at an even greater pace than before. "It's gonna be soon."

"What consequences?" Greg asked. He was really warming to the idea of a world without his father in it. Especially one where he'd never even existed. His mother wouldn't know to be sad, or to grieve him.

Amélie growled before answering. "Come on…" She stopped short, making Greg run right into her back. "What's your name again?"

"Greg," he said.

She nodded, then took off again. "Come on, Greg. You seem like a smart guy. Think about it."

Greg was thinking about it. It seemed absolutely brilliant. "What if you go through and ask to remove Hitler."

Amélie rolled her eyes. "Want to make a guess as to the number of people who have done just that?"

"Many?"

"Thousands."

She was slowing down, allowing Greg to catch up and walk next to her. They'd entered a large square, large enough to house the entire village he'd stopped in the night before.

In the center, in front of a wide staircase shaped like an amphitheater leading down to a Fnac store, stood a bubble the size of a small building.

It really was like the bubbles the girl next door had blown all through the summer between the fourth and the fifth grade. Transparent, but when the sunlight hit at a certain angle, colorful shapes moved across the surface, like rainbow colored eels playing hide and seek.

On the ground, a fence had been set up, keeping people away from the bubble. The only hole in the fence was a tiny cabin, with a line of four people in front of it. Behind them, two police officers stood guard, though they seemed bored.

"You've really never seen one before, huh?" Amélie said.

Greg realized they'd completely stopped, and he'd probably stood there staring like an idiot for several minutes.

"That's cool," she said lightly. "I mean, they only exist in Grenoble, so if you've never been…"

"So what does this one do?" he asked.

Amélie scowled at the bubble. "It's the one I was talking about. To erase a person's very existence."

Greg's feet moved forward, as if of their own accord.

"Greg!" Amélie caught up with him and grabbed his elbow. "You do not want to use that one. No matter what someone has done to you."

It's not just me, Greg thought as he dragged Amélie along with him toward the little cabin.

"Have you ever read that book by Stephen King?" Amélie asked. "The one where a guy goes back in time to stop the JFK murder?"

Greg shook his head.

"It's this really, really long book," she said. "For, like, five hundred pages, this guy's only goal is to get to the killer before he pulls the trigger. You read along, wondering if he's going to pull it off or not. Usually, the conclusion of stories like that is that you can't change the past."

Greg slowed for a second to glance at the girl hanging onto his elbow.

"What?" she said. "I'm interested in the subject. I've read a lot of books on time travel. Sue me. Anyway, in this book, he actually does manage to save JFK. And can you guess what happens?"

"I'd say the world is a better place," Greg said. He didn't really know much about American history, but he'd heard enough about that particular incident to know everybody considered it a catastrophe for humanity.

"See, that's not what happens in the book. JFK lives, but everything else goes to hell, and when the guy comes back to today, the world is about to go under. And it makes perfect sense."

Greg stopped to face Amélie. "So the world ends at the end of the book?"

Amélie glanced at the bubble, now only twenty meters away, before locking her gaze on Greg. "Well, Stephen King is the king of horror. But no. The guy goes back in time again to reset everything, lets JFK get killed, and calls it a day."

Greg frowned. "That's kind of anticlimactic."

"I'll lend you the book," Amélie said. "You'll see. And the point here is that the people who go through asking for Hitler to never have been born? I'm far from convinced they're going to a better place. Maybe Hitler coming to power meant that someone even worse wasn't able to. Maybe that other guy would have won the war, and we'd all be living under the rule of the Third Reich right now."

Greg frowned at her. It had sounded like such a good idea. But she was, unfortunately, making sense. Still, he didn't have to aim that high…

Amélie grabbed Greg's shoulders and shook him. "I can see what you're thinking, Greg. Stop it, right this minute. No matter who you're going for. Think about the consequences of removing just one person from the world. Like this one guy who was so frustrated by his father-in-law never warming to him. So he went through requesting the man never existed."

"What happened?" Greg asked.

"Well, I don't actually know, do I?" Amélie gave him a stern glare. "Nobody knows what happens once people go through. They never come back to tell us. But that one should be obvious. Tell me, Greg. If I remove the father from a family, how many kids do you think the mother will have, all on her own?"

Greg's breath caught. "It removes the kids?"

"Of course it does! The guy was never there to conceive the child!"

"So the guy went to a world where his father-in-law never existed, but then neither did his wife?"

"Now you're getting it. Seriously, that one is so dangerous. There's just no way to anticipate what might be changed by your request."

Greg stared longingly at the bubble towering above them. The oily colors swirled and shifted.

Damn her for making sense.

"Can I just go have a closer look?" he asked.

"Fine," Amélie conceded. "But I'm coming with you." She grabbed his hand and squeezed hard enough to make Greg wince.

As they reached the wooden cabin by the bubble, a man emerged from a door at its back. He was rather on the short side, had balding blond hair, and an angry scowl. He stepped right up to the bubble, then seemed to hesitate.

"Is he going through?" Greg asked. "How does it work?"

"All you need is for your skin to touch the bubble," Amélie said. "Then on this side you go poof, and you'll appear in the other world."

"But nobody ever comes back?"

She shook her head.

"Then how do we know how it works? How can we be sure the people don't just cease to exist? Or even if they work, that they work the way you say they do."

Amélie's gaze was on the man in front of the bubble, but Greg didn't think she was actually seeing him. "I just know. I can feel it."

The man reached out toward the roiling surface of the bubble. His hand touched the surface.

He disappeared.

No popping sound, no flash, no nothing.

"That's also kind of anticlimactic," Greg said.

The three persons still waiting in line exchanged excited glances. They were clearly waiting for it to be their turn. The police officers scanned the crowd, making Greg think this might be the moment when someone could possibly try to do something dangerous or illegal.

Greg locked eyes with one of the officers for a second, before the man turned to say something to his colleague.

"He won't be any better off on the other side," Amélie said, still that distant look on her face, as if she was listening to something only she could hear.

It didn't feel like she was theorizing. "How do you know?" Greg asked.

"I can feel it," she explained. "Some of us just can." Her eyes scanned the circumference of the bubble and she sighed. "I can feel what you can wish for, and I can feel a remnant of what the people who go through feel about the world they've arrived in.

"Some bubbles give mostly positive results. For example, there's this one tiny red bubble that allows you to undo one action you regret. If you don't go too far back in time and choose something that will have minimum impact—for example, just on you and one other person—you can come out a winner."

Her eyes still on the bubble, Amélie suddenly winced. She started moving away, pulling Greg along by the hand. "Come on, let's go."

"What happened?"

"He realized he'd have been better off not going through,"

Amélie said. "Like ninety-nine percent of the people who use this one."

As they passed the cabin, Greg caught a glimpse of a poster on one of its walls.

"Two thousand euros! That's insane!"

"That's the cost of entering a parallel universe," Amélie said. She was pulling Greg along toward a narrow street winding away from the far corner of the square.

"It should be expensive, by the way," she added. "Or everyone would go through on a whim and we'd have nobody left on this side."

Greg would have no choice but to stay on this side if that was how much it cost to pass through. He now had less than eighty euros, and no way to get any more.

His feelings must have shown on his face because Amélie stopped just as they entered the narrow street and gave him a hug. "Don't worry, Greg. We'll figure something out. Maybe we could make things better for you in this world?"

Tears threatened, but Greg fought them back. He was not going to cry in front of this girl. And he was not going to cry out of self-pity; that was in the past. The present Greg had a plan, and he was going to go through with it.

He was about to tell Amélie as much when she suddenly jerked and her head snapped up, her gaze going to the sky.

"There's a new one," she whispered.

"A new what?"

"A new bubble. It's been brewing for days. Even the people who usually can't feel a thing have known this one was coming."

She took off down the street—la Grande Rue according to a plate on the wall—once again pulling Greg along for the ride.

"Come on," she said. "I need to know what it does."

Greg hurried to keep up. "I thought you didn't like people using them."

"Which is why I need to know what it does. Whenever a new bubble appears, there's always some idiot who goes through completely blind, not caring what it does, just that it's free until the city can set up a perimeter."

After a turn and another narrow cobbled street lined with tall stone buildings, Amélie brought them to a stop in a public park. On their left stood a preschool with a tiny courtyard, and on their right, just across the river, the Bastille rose into the mist.

"They always appear near the Bastille," Amélie said. She seemed to be scanning the rose bushes in the park as she talked. "We've not understood the significance of the mountain yet, but it plays some sort of role, that's for sure."

She went down on all fours and crawled along the path next to a bush of yellow roses. "Why is it so hard to find?" she muttered to herself. "My entire body is humming with the power. I can't believe it's a small one. Ah—here it is."

She whisked a pair of rubber gloves out of the front pocket of her jeans and snapped them on. Very carefully, she inserted a hand into the rose bush. It came back with a bright pink bubble the size of a ping pong ball.

"Should you be touching that?" After all her speeches, Greg couldn't understand why she would risk passing through on accident.

"It needs to be in contact with your skin for it to take you away," Amélie explained. "Any kid could find it in there. It's not safe to let them lie just anywhere."

"Then why haven't they moved the one we saw earlier?"

Amélie sat down on a bench on the other side of the path and brought the ball up to eye level.

"Because it's too big to move without risk," she said. "And it's been secured. And it's a major tourist attraction. So the city is just fine with it staying put."

"They all belong to the city?" Greg sat down on the bench next to Amélie and dropped his backpack to the ground. His t-shirt was still as disgustingly soaked as earlier, but at least his lungs seemed to have adapted somewhat to the climate.

"Yes," Amélie replied. "At first it was a first arrived, first served kind of thing, but that got out of hand real quick, and a law was passed to give ownership to the city where the bubble first appeared."

"I thought this only happened in Grenoble."

Amélie winked. "It does. But in case it starts somewhere else, the law is ready for it."

"Should you be moving it around? Won't the city mind?"

Amélie was rolling the ball from the palm of one hand to the other. Though it was pink and opaque, it wasn't just one color. Like with the larger bubble earlier, there were shapes shifting around on the surface, except they were hundreds of different hues of pink. It was mesmerizing.

"It's fine," she said absently. "I've done this before."

She had a portal to a different world in the palm of her hand.

If Greg reached out and touched it, he would be transported somewhere else. Somewhere very similar to this world, but with one thing different.

"So what does it do?" he asked. Greg was starting to understand the need for the city to protect the new bubbles. The temptation to just reach out and get the pass for free was overwhelming. Who cared what it did. He just needed to wish for something to change with his dad, and the other side was bound to be an improvement.

"Working on it." Amélie kept rolling the ball between her hands, sometimes blowing on it, sometimes holding it close to her ear to listen.

"In a way it seems very similar to the big one on Place Grenette." The frown on Amélie's forehead showed how little she liked that idea. "But it's also the complete opposite."

"Okay…"

Amélie brought the bubble up right in front of her nose. Her eyes crossed a little as she stared at the moving lines.

"The action is on the existence of the person you place your wish on." She shook her head. "But I don't feel the destruction that oozes out of the other one."

Greg had trouble following. He could reach out, wish for his father to disappear, and he'd be golden.

A hand clamped down on his. "Don't you dare!" Amélie hissed. "Not before we know what it does. Actually, probably not even then. These things are not benign."

"Maybe some of them are," Greg argued. "You just haven't run into any of the constructive ones yet."

Amélie drew in a sharp breath. "That's it. It creates instead of destroys."

"Huh?"

Amélie's eyes went wide and she regarded the pink bubble with an awe Greg wouldn't have thought her capable of.

"You wish for someone to exist, and you end up in a world where they do."

"Like bringing someone back to life?"

"No," she whispered. "Like wishing for your soul mate to exist, and then he does."

Movement caught Greg's attention. Two police officers—seemed like the two who'd been guarding the bubble earlier—were approaching down the path.

"Grégoire Lefebvre?" one of them asked.

Greg froze.

"Oh, shit," Amélie whispered. The hand holding the bubble lowered to her lap and she seemed to be looking at Greg a lot more closely than she had up until then. "You're that kid who disappeared in Lyon three days ago. I knew your face rang a bell."

The officers stood in front of the bench, effectively closing off all escape routes. "Your parents have been worried sick looking for you, young man," the first officer said.

"My…parents?" Greg's voice cracked on the last word.

"Yes, your parents. They should be here shortly. They weren't too far away since they spent the night in the village you apparently went through yesterday."

"Grégoire!" His dad's voice must have been heard by half the city. He came striding across the park, his huge arms swinging and his brows drawn together in a dangerous line.

Greg tried to make a run for it, but the officers anticipated him.

"Running will only make it worse," the one holding him in place said under his breath.

"Well," Greg's dad said in a tone that promised a lot of unpleasant things once they got home, "I wish I could say I was surprised. I'm not. You keep doing your best to be a disappointment to your mother and I, and I think it's the one thing we can count on you to excel at."

Amélie's eyes jumped between Greg and his dad, understanding dawning. Luckily, she didn't say anything.

That would only have made things worse.

She did, however, get up to stand next to Greg. She still held the bubble, but she'd curled her fingers around it protectively. Greg didn't think his father or the police officers realized what she was holding.

Greg's dad stalked up to stand in front of Greg, towering over him.

"I wish I'd had a different son," he said.

Greg saw a flash of pink and heard Amélie gasp. The bubble crashed into his dad's face and popped on impact.

"I'm so sorry!" Amélie yelled. "I didn't think!" She brought her hands up to her mouth, but when Greg's dad didn't disappear, she slowly lowered them.

"Come on, Dad," a male voice said from behind Greg. "Calm down, will you? He just needed a break. I knew where he was the whole time."

Greg turned, as if in slow motion, to face…his brother.

He'd never had a brother. He was an only child.

Except…he wasn't.

The information tore through his brain like a tidal wave. For a while, he could remember both hiding alone in the garden shed when his dad was angry and looking for him and hanging out in his brother's room because his big brother was taking care of him while his dad was busy with work.

It worked its way through his entire life and left behind a completely different boy with completely different memories. He still had the ghost of a memory of what had just happened.

"It's completely reversed," Amélie whispered to herself. "Everything is backwards. Oh God, this changes everything."

She grabbed Greg's face with both hands and stared into his eyes. "Greg, how do you feel?"

"Great," Greg replied. "I feel great." He really did.

Like he always did when he hung out with his brother.

THE LUCIA CROWN

I don't scare easily. When my friends and classmates freak out, I stay calm, cool, and collected.

But when it comes to the Lucia Crown, I'm terrified. I've never wanted anything more than to be Saint Lucia at the concert, leading the choir through the school gym while wearing the coveted crown of candles.

We're going to vote on it. Sounds easy enough, right? But when the voters are unpredictable teens, nothing is easy.

ONE

I DON'T SCARE easily. When all my classmates were freaking in June because the Maths syllabus was so huge, I simply hunkered down, split the thing into more manageable pieces, and set to work. When we go cross-country skiing and we get to that beak-neck downhill toward the end, I don't attempt to brake to be in full control all the way down. I know there's a tiny uphill after that will help me to stop once I reach the bottom, and in the meantime…that descent is such a rush. When I had to read my latest essay in front of the class because the teacher thought it was "profound," I did it with a firm voice and without showing any doubt.

But today we're having a vote about who gets to walk around with a wreath of candles on her head for half an hour—and I'm terrified.

Why? Because I want it too much.

Tomorrow is December 13th, Santa Lucia. Our choir is

having a huge concert in the school's gym and all two hundred tickets are already sold out. We're doing our usual repertoire of songs and adding in some mandatory Christmas songs since it's just two weeks before the big day.

And then we're doing Lucia.

It's just the one song, and it's not very long, only three verses. But it's the big, final act. It's the concert's culminating moment and the one that always makes my heart soar.

I love the song, its message of light showing way in the darkness, the way it goes so high the altos have trouble hitting the notes at times, and so low it's the sopranos who suffer. I love the visuals the choir always offers, with everyone in white robes that we borrow from the church for the day, everyone over the age of thirteen with live candles in their hands, and the visual effects the lighting team keeps getting better at every year.

And Santa Lucia. Every year, one girl is elected to represent the saint. She stands a step ahead of the rest of the choir, dressed in the same white robes, but with a wreath of lights in her hair. And she leads the procession that will take us all off stage and across the gym to the exit.

This is my last year with a chance at the role. Actually, it's also the first. Lucia is always one of the high school seniors. We all get just the *one* shot.

The children's choir will also be part of this one song, which is why they've been brought in to vote for the Lucia. I remember how proud I was when I was allowed to vote, to give my voice to who would be the most beautiful representation of the saint. I always had my favorite and sat there staring at the girl in question the whole time we were there, hoping she would notice me.

I see quite a few of the young girls around us doing the same right now. The boys, for the most part, are pretending to be above such silliness and are playing games on their phones. The ones who don't have phones lean in to do commentary on their friends' conquests.

I think a few of the girls are looking at me. Maybe. I did let my hair out of its usual bun on purpose and brushed it to a golden shine before coming.

People tend to like having blonde long-haired Lucias. I don't personally agree that she should be blonde but I'm also not above using it to my advantage, just this once.

I'm pretty sure several of the girls are looking at Nina, though, and not at me. Maybe.

Nina is my best friend and has sung in this choir for one week longer than me. We were both ten and when I first arrived, I was completely lost. Nina, with her one week's worth of experience, showed me around. I basically haven't let her out of my sight since.

Nina *isn't* blonde. She was adopted from South-Korea when she was a baby so even though she sounds and behaves as Norwegian as you can get, physically, she's very different. I find her petite stature, narrow black eyes, and sleek black hair gorgeous, but I don't think she'll get enough votes to be Lucia. I don't think this group is quite there yet.

She's getting *my* vote, of course. If I can't be Lucia, it has to be Nina.

They've set up a new system for voting this year. We're going through some website and everyone can vote using their phones. Then there's a visual representation of our votes on a screen. Seems fun in theory, at least.

"All right, people," Kristin, our director, yells to get everyone to settle down. "We're ready for the vote. When I open the poll, you can type in the name of the girl you want for Lucia. After five minutes, we'll see which three names appear the most often and then have a vote on those three."

"Why only girls?" Perry yells from the back. He's the undisputed king of our high school and should be too cool to be part of a choir but he has the voice of an angel and knows it and has somehow managed to become king of this place too and still stay cool.

I stay as far away from him as I can.

Kristin rolls her eyes. "You can vote for boys, too, if you want. I'm sure you'd look very pretty with a wreath of candles in your hair, Perry."

"Oh, I wasn't thinking about me." And he sends a meaningful glance at Marius.

Marius, who is not very big, not very strong, who makes rumors about him being gay flare every time he does something that doesn't fit with the masculine stereotype. Like singing in a choir.

Talk about double standards.

"People better not follow that jerk's lead," Nina mutters.

Kristin doesn't so much as look at Marius but I see her swallow. "Nobody will be forced to play Lucia. If the winner doesn't want the honors, the runner-up will get the crown. Let's vote."

We all bend over our phones. It's only possible to vote once, so I send in my vote for Nina. As I glance over at my friend, I see her typing in my name. My heart does a little jump in my chest.

On the screen, the votes are appearing in colorful bubbles. Kristin moves them around in clusters, grouping the votes for the same person.

I see several with my own name, quite a few of Nina's—and too many of Marius's.

"All the guys are voting for Marius, aren't they?" I whisper to Nina.

"All right," Kristin says. "All the votes are in." She takes a deep breath. "Before we move to the second round…Marius, do you want us to keep your name in the race?"

I can't see the exact count, but the poor guy wins with quite the margin.

All heads turn to look at Marius. I know he doesn't like the attention but I also can't *not* look at him.

My heart breaks a little when I see his face. He's beet red and clearly would like to be anywhere else but here…but I also think he'd actually like to be Lucia. Girls aren't the only ones who might find the tradition magical.

He shakes his head with jerky movements. Perry and his cronies snicker.

Kristin ignores them. "So Marius is out of the race. This means we'll have a final vote between Aurora, Nina, and Tuva."

Tuva doesn't stand a chance. She only got five votes in the first round and those were from her group of friends, guaranteed. So it's basically between me and my best friend.

I reach out to hold her hand, suddenly needing the reassurance that this won't ruin our friendship.

"Are you making up drama in your head again?" Nina asks.

"Yes."

"Okay." She squeezes my hand and grabs her phone in the other. "I'm voting for you."

I have the worst time unlocking and handling my phone with my left hand but I manage to vote for Nina before the time is up.

As we wait for the vote to finish, my hand is still in Nina's and I'm increasingly aware of that fact. We don't hold hands very often, and if we do, it's for a second or two in passing. This has been going on for a solid minute. And my hand is getting sweaty. My heart is jittery and it's not even for the election.

"Everybody got their votes in?" Kristin gives us half a second to reply before clicking on the "Results" button. "Our next Lucia is…"

My name pops up on the screen.

There's no score so I don't know by how much I won. I'm *glad* I don't know. But I *won*! And Nina *lost*.

Feeling both insanely happy and sorely disappointed at once is very confusing.

Nina hugging me close and congratulating me doesn't help. She smells of lavender from the shampoo I gave her for her birthday last month. I knew that scent would suit her.

I take one deep lungful then extricate myself and smile at all the young girls from the children's' choir.

I'm going to be Lucia.

TWO

THE DAY OF the concert, Friday the thirteenth, backstage in the school gym: complete and utter chaos.

There are nineteen kids, ages ten to thirteen, running around in white robes, with silver tinsel in their hair and each carrying a fake electrical candle, some turning it on and off over and over until Kristin yells at them.

The twelve boys from our choir prance around in their robes, making jokes and blustering in order to cover the fact that they're wearing something that's a little too close to a dress for their comfort. They tell Kristin—just like they did last year and every year before that—that no, they will not wear tinsel in their hair. They will, however, take the candles, I suspect only because it means they're allowed to play with an open flame. Whoever thought *that* was a good idea is an idiot.

The older girls, all twenty-five of us, also have live candles. One girl out of three has a lighter so that we can light up when the time comes. Some have made intricate wreaths of the tinsel they were given, some have weaved it into their braids. Nina is absolutely magnificent with a braid going around her head like a crown and the silver tinsel braided in, making is seem like she has sparkly silver highlights. Her mother is a genius with those braids she always does for her daughter.

My hair is free and cascading down my back. I spent twenty minutes brushing it before coming here. I am going to be the best Santa Lucia *ever*.

"Where's your wreath?" Kristin asks me. Her eyes are a little wild and only the left half of her hair is still inside her ponytail. I don't think it's a fashion statement.

"Uh. I haven't seen it yet. I thought you would bring it to me."

Kristin takes a deep breath and lets it out, slowly. "Every year it's the same thing." She points to the boxes in the back, where all the tinsel and lights have been coming from. "It's in one of those boxes with the rest of the stuff. You're the Lucia; you go find it."

I scurry over to the boxes and start looking through them.

Nina joins me. "What are we looking for?" She's going through a box before I even answer.

"The Lucia wreath."

"Oh! Yeah, might be a good idea to find that one. You know, before the concert starts."

"Not helping."

The concert is scheduled to start in fifteen minutes and the two first boxes yield nothing but tinsel and lights. Next four boxes: same thing.

The wreath isn't in any of the boxes.

"Somebody has already taken it out of the box." I spin around slowly in a circle, really looking at everyone, seeing if anyone has put the Lucia wreath on their own head or if one of the young girls is playing with it.

There are lots of lights but none attached to a wreath made of branches. That thing is the only thing made of wood in the entire procession.

"Perry and his clique aren't here," Nina says.

"Neither is Marius," I say.

Our gazes meet for a second. "We need to find Perry."

A quick look behind the curtain shows the gym filling up with parents but no white figures with a wreath. We work on the assumption that the boys will still be wearing their robes because even if they like causing mayhem, they will not want to actually ruin the concert. They take as much pride in our performance as the rest of us.

We quickly run through the three rooms backstage—nobody there.

Across the lobby and down the hallway to the changing rooms. We pop our heads into the girls' room; empty.

Nina stops in front of the boys' locker room, her hand on the door handle. "We're not allowed in there. We're not boys."

"Nobody's supposed to be changing now. And this is an emergency." I put my hand over hers, feel a little zing shooting up my arm, and pull the door open.

My first thought: I was too quick to accuse Perry.

My second: Wait, no. It *is* Perry.

Marius is standing on one of the benches along the far wall, wearing his white robe, one unlit candle in each hand, tinsel making a criss-crossing pattern across his torso—and the Lucia wreath on his head.

And on our side of the room, with their backs to us, Perry and his clique.

They're holding up their phones, taking pictures of Marius. "Just one more picture, Marius. A couple more seconds and your pretty face will remain unblemished."

Nina rushes through the door, her eyes alight like a beautiful, dark angel. "I'm so happy to learn that you agree he has a pretty face, Perry. What is it about it that you like so much? The cheekbones? The full lips? The blue eyes?"

A small part of my brain is blaring red alert alarms. There are four rather big boys in the room; a group that I *know* like to bully others and don't mind throwing in a fist or two. Then there's Nina and myself; two girls who stopped growing at thirteen. And Marius. The poor boy is frozen in fear on that bench and won't be a help to anybody until someone manages to reboot him.

But where my normal reaction in this situation would be to run away, to get as much distance between me and the danger as possible, I now have an additional element to consider: Nina, standing on tiptoe in front of Perry, squaring off.

I can't let her do this on her own. I will not allow Perry to put any blemishes on *her* skin.

So with absolutely no forethought, I barge into the locker room, finger wagging like I'm an angry grandmother who caught her grandson with his dirty fingers in the cookie dough.

"Perry, what the hell do you think you're doing? Why are you torturing Marius like that? Don't you know the concert starts in, like, five minutes? Seriously, how old are you? Five? You're eighteen, dude! You're supposed to behave like a goddamned adult!"

I'm in his face, right next to Nina, and together we're forming a very angry female wall that reaches Perry's chin, approximately.

I start to run out of steam but Perry is wide-eyed and clearly in shock that someone is standing up to him, a situation I need to take full advantage of.

I swerve to the right to go up to Marius and pull him down from the bench. "Come on, Marius. We're out of here. Let's go get ready for the concert." As we pass the group of bullies, I once again point my finger at Perry. "Kristin will hear of this."

Shouldn't have said that. Heat rises in Perry's cheeks and his chest visibly inflates as he prepares his counter-attack.

Time to retreat. I grab Nina with my free hand and pull all three of us out the locker room door and down the hall toward the gym.

We run into Kristin backstage. Her ponytail has disappeared completely and a sheen of sweat is visible both on her forehead and on her neck. "Where were you guys? We're about to start. Marius! Why are you wearing the wreath?"

I yank the wreath off Marius's head and put in on mine. "Don't worry, Kristin. We're ready." I pull the tinsels off Marius's body, probably hurting him in the process but not caring.

As we run for the stage, I hear Perry and his goons exiting the locker room and Kristin swearing under her breath when she puts two and two together.

THREE

I'M NOT SUPPOSED to actually wear the crown until the Lucia song at the end, so I pull it off as we take our places on the soprano side of the choir. The plan was for me to put the wreath off to the side behind the curtain but the murderous look on Perry's face when he takes up his spot in the back makes me change my mind. I keep it in my hand and hold my hands behind my back so the audience won't see it.

The concert is great. Not a single false start or off-tune note in sight and Kristin visibly relaxes as we plow through our repertoire and the audience obviously loves everything.

Then it's time for the Santa Lucia song.

The lights are dimmed so we can only see each other's white robes and the emergency exit lights. The audience, who knows the drill, keeps quiet.

The children's' choir, who have somehow managed to stay calm in the back rooms during the entire concert, march out and take up their places in front of us. They each have their fake candles lit, giving them a very soft glow just strong enough to light up their little faces.

And I step up to the very front, putting the crown on my head but leaving it unlit.

Kristin counts down from three, and the children start singing.

"*Svart senker natten seg…*"

While they sing of the black night, the room stays dark. I reach up to the wreath, finding the switch that will turn on the lights. God, I wish I'd had the time to test it before coming on stage.

As the children start the line where Lucia appears, I flip the switch.

The wreath lights up.

We do this every year and the audience is pretty much the same every year, since it's mostly our parents, friends, and relatives. And yet, every year, there's a general intake of breath when the Lucia appears.

This year is no exception.

For the second verse, the girls in our choir join in. They quickly light their candles and the light surges in synch with the volume of the song.

I also light my candle but I don't sing. I'm just to stand there and look serene as I light the way through the darkness.

I see several hands on hearts and glittering eyes in the audience, including my parents out on the right wing.

For the third and final verse, the boys join in. More lights, more volume. More depth, especially with Perry's beautiful tenor carrying us all to new heights.

This is what I always associate with singing in a choir. This magical moment, with the beautiful song starting out low in the belly and finishing off way up in the clouds. The feeling of being part of a group, being carried by a team.

And this year I get to be the central figure, like I always dreamed of.

The last notes taper off and the gym is left in silence. One newbie parent starts applauding but is quickly silenced by his neighbors. Most of them know the drill.

It's time for the procession.

The youngest children swarm forward and form two lines, one going past on each side of me. They walk carefully down the stairs leading down from the stage and start down the aisle separating the audience in two.

I'm next, then the rest of the choir. Nina comes in right behind me, on the right. On the left…Perry.

How did he manage to make his way up front from his spot at the very back?

No matter. I have a job to do.

I walk carefully down the short flight of stairs, taking care not to move my head too much for fear the crown will fall off—that happened to one girl three years ago and I will *not* make the same mistake—and proceed down the aisle after the children.

When they reach the last row of the audience, they scatter in all directions. It's officially the end of the procession. They have very strict instructions to stay quiet until everybody has arrived but they're allowed to move.

As I reach the end, I let out a breath I must have been holding in since I left the stage. I did it. I was Lucia and it was *awesome*.

The next thirty seconds feel like they last thirty minutes. I'm not even sure I understand what happens.

There's the smell of something burning.

Nina yelling, "What the hell—!"

One of the girls behind me exclaiming, "Oh my god!" in that tone that's supposed to be shocked but is actually closer to gleefully thrilled.

And Perry's, "Oops." Plus a chuckle.

Next thing I know, I'm lying on the floor with Nina straddling my waist. The crown goes flying and I hear a crunching sound that must be from at least one of the candles breaking.

Nina is hitting me.

Wait, no.

She's hitting something right next to my head.

My hair.

"There," Nina says, still banging her flat palm on my hair spread out on the floor. "It's out. I think. You!" She pulls on the coattails of a woman walking past. "Give me your water!" She grabs the woman's half-empty water bottle and empties it on my hair. And my face.

I blink, several times, trying to get the water out of my eyes. Only now do I notice that Nina has my arms pinned to my side and I cannot move.

"I'm so sorry," Nina babbles. She runs her hand over my face, wiping away the water. Her eyes widen. "Oh shit, your mascara."

As she bends down to see better and draws one finger gently under my left eye, I'm surrounded by her lavender scent, with just a touch of singed hair. I should care about the hair part, I really should.

But all I can think about is how close she is. How intently she's staring at my face as she cleans it up. How soft her lips look.

"Perry!" Kristin's shout makes me jerk so hard I manage to free one hand and Nina almost pokes my eye out.

"That is the *last* straw! You will not show your face in this choir ever again, you hear me? Your parents are going to hear about this! Oh, wait. Are they here? Are Perry's parents here tonight? Where? I want them."

I don't actually see any of the drama going on around me. I only see Nina's widening eyes and her hand shaking so badly I'm afraid she might have another stab at my eye—literally.

I grab her shaking hand with my free one and pull them out of my line of sight. "Nina?" I say softly. "We need to get up before someone steps on us."

We are, after all, lying flat on the floor in the middle of a crowd of more than two hundred people. Just to be on the safe side, we're in the direct path of anyone who wants to reach the sweets being set out on a table in the back.

Nina scrambles off me, kneeing me in the thigh, and I jump up after her. She's about to run off, but I hold her back. I haven't let go of her hand.

"Wait," I say. "How bad is my hair?"

At the moment, I don't really care that much, but I know that's going to change once the adrenaline wears off. Still, it can't be that bad. I see hair everywhere and can already tell it's going to take me hours to get all the knots out tonight.

Getting Nina to focus on my problems was the right thing to do. Her eyes come back into focus as she gingerly pulls the hair from my back over my right shoulder. "He set fire to the part in the middle of your back. But it didn't get very far up before we stopped it." She holds up a strand of hair with blackened and curled ends. The burnt smell from earlier returns.

Sighing, I grab the hair. Pull out some that hasn't been burned.

I'm missing about ten centimeters.

Kind of a lot but then I had a lot to begin with.

"Guess I'll be getting a haircut," I say. I try to sound casual but my voice breaks a little on the last word. Dammit.

Nina gently pulls the singed hair out of my hands and moves it back out of sight. Then she finger-brushes the rest, pushing it out of my face and generally doing her best to make me presentable.

Marius comes up to us, the broken wreath in one hand. "You dropped this," he says.

"Right." I look at the poor thing. Two of the six candles are broken and the wreath itself seems to be somewhat bent out of shape. "I don't…" I recognize the look in his eyes suddenly. It's the way I looked at that thing every single year up until now. "Maybe you should hold on to it until Kristin needs it again?"

"I don't…"

"Maybe you could fix the candles," Nina says. "Someone needs to get on that."

Marius knows what we're doing but I'm happy see him come to the conclusion that he doesn't care. Perry hasn't broken him yet. Nodding, he walks off toward the stage, cradling the wreath against his chest.

"How about some lussekatter?" Nina asks, her beautiful dark eyes staring straight into mine.

There are two great things about Santa Lucia. One is the song with the lights and the crown and the tassels. The other is the lussekatter. The special buns made with dried raisins and saffron. The saffron makes them yellow—apparently a trick to scare away the devil. Also works for attracting hungry girls.

Grabbing Nina's hand again, I pull her toward the table. "Great idea," I say. I grab four buns, ignoring the glare of the mother standing behind the table, and cradle them against my chest. "How about we take them to go? My house is empty right now."

My eyes widen at the same time as Nina's. Seems like none of us expected me to issue that challenge.

Nina takes it, though. "Sounds great." Then she squeezes my hand.

LET THEM EAT CAKE

Being the outcast in school is never fun, as Elisabeth knows only too well.

Nobody ever takes your side. Nobody ever defends you.

And nobody hesitates to accuse you when a crime has been committed.

Twenty-five fourteen-year-olds make a certain amount of noise, even while trying to be quiet at eight in the morning.

The class is waiting for our teacher to arrive and we've all hung our denim jackets on the hooks lining the walls, each person always using the same hook from day to day or we'd probably never figure out which jacket belongs to who. Mine is just a hint darker than the rest of them, but it's not a ploy to stand out. It's my mother's unwillingness to part with an extra fifty bucks for *just* the right color.

We've dumped our backpacks along the walls. We have Maths, Science, *and* English today, so the damn things weigh as much as a dead donkey. I smile at myself at the thought—that's one of my favorite French expressions. It always makes me imagine a dead donkey in place of my stupidly non-cool backpack.

The cool boys are pushing each other around up by the window at the end of the hall, like they always do, and I wonder what the point is, like I always do.

The uncool boys hunch over one guy's phone, probably checking out yet another new game, or better yet, the video of a guy playing a game. That one I'll never understand.

The cool girls are—wait for it—whispering, giggling, and gossiping. Okay, I'm not actually close enough to hear what they're saying, but it's a universally known fact that when you put several cool girls together, they gossip. Probably about me. Or they may be pretending I don't exist today. Too early to tell yet.

The uncool girls…well, that would be me. And I'm not a plural, just singular little me.

I'm keeping my distance, fiddling with my phone, pretending to have important stuff to check out. I'm actually just flipping back and forth through the pages of my welcome screen, watching the colors flash by. I don't even watch videos of other people doing interesting stuff because all my focus is on my peripheral vision, making sure there are no imminent threats.

Here's to hoping high school will be better.

Our teacher, Mr. Pedersen, comes through the door at the other end of the building. All the other classes have already entered their classrooms, so he's walking down an empty hallway, but Mr. Pedersen is not one to speed up for anything. He's the youngest teacher in school—I think he's twenty-six—and the girls from the other classes are *so* jealous of our teacher.

Sure, he's handsome enough and sure, he's a nice guy. But seriously, are they expecting him to be interested in them or something? I don't think saying that's never going to happen is me being pessimistic. And they don't have to sludge through his classes every day, counting the dust motes swirling around in the classroom while he explains for the hundredth time how to draw a sixty degree angle using a pair of compasses.

Seriously, I think we understood how to do that at Christmas.

But no, Marie calls him over every day, asking him to explain it to her again. As if leaning into her cloud of stifling perfume enough times is going to make the teacher fall for her.

Him dropping dead from the stench is more likely.

"All right, kids," Mr. Pedersen says as he searches his pockets for his keys. "Time to calm down."

The noise stays the same, of course.

Mr. Pedersen opens the classroom door and steps inside. I grab my backpack and my classmates do the same. The cool boys continue shoving each other, the uncool boys still stare at their phones, and Marie and her clique are exchanging knowing glances.

I'm the last one through the door. But where I can usually make a beeline for my seat in the back, today I can only see a mass of bodies and backpacks. Being short is such a blast.

"Who did this?" Mr. Pedersen's tone is…odd. Not his usual nonchalance with a hint of a smile, but something much more strained. And angry. In the almost two years he's been our teacher, he's never been angry once. Not when Marie does one of her stunts, not when Robert smashed the glass door to the cabinets in the back while playing soccer in the classroom, and not when Daniel was caught cheating on a Maths exam.

One of the guys utters an admiring, "Dude!" and another exclaims, "That's so gross."

Daniel, who's been blocking my view, spins to face me, his face completely white and his eyes wide. Without even seeing me, he runs past me to get back out in the corridor. I think I hear him throw up out there.

Despite my general dislike of being in the middle of a group, I step into the space Daniel vacated, to see what made him go green around the gills.

So much blood.

Most of the first row of desks are covered with it, and a good part of the teacher's desk, too.

Something lies sprawled on the middle desk, Marie's, and next to it stands some sort of wooden contraption. With a blade.

"It's a cat," I say stupidly. A dead cat on Marie's desk.

"No shit, Sherlock," Marie says from her position next to Mr. Pedersen.

I shoot her a withering look, but don't bother with a comeback.

"The head's on the floor." This from Robert, who's walked around the bloody mess to the far corner of the classroom. He points to the floor by the teacher's desk. "Somebody decapitated a cat." His grin goes from ear to ear.

Stupid boys.

But I realize he's right. The poor thing on Marie's desk is indeed a headless cat.

Who would do such a thing?

"Somebody *guillotined* a cat," Marie says, voice as calm as ever, her head held in that up-tilted arrogant way she has, as if she's the queen and everybody else her worthless underlings.

She's right, though. That wooden contraption? A DIY guillotine.

They'd taken a wooden crate and removed the bottom to get a rectangular base. A large cleaver was attached to a stone—probably to make sure it's heavy enough—and tied to the top of the crate. Well, it must have been attached to the top at the start, but now it stands buried in the bottom of the crate, so far in I feel certain it must also have created a dent in the desk.

A guillotine.

We'd discussed those in French class just last week. We'd all been fascinated by the morbid history of the thing, and the way it had ended the life of the eccentric Marie Antoinette. No more cake for her.

"Don't touch that!" Mr. Pedersen's voice booms through the classroom, making me jump.

Robert stops in a half-crouched position, his hand stretched out toward what I assume is the poor cat's head on the floor.

"Jesus, Robert," Mr. Pedersen fumes. "You're not three. Show some restraint."

Robert straightens, and his cheeks turn pink, but he keeps glancing to the floor. Yeah, he'll go for it again if the teacher ever turns his back.

Mr. Pedersen must have realized the same thing. "Robert, you take all the boys with you and go to the Dean's office."

The injustice on Robert's face is almost comical. "But—"

"I'm not sending *you* to the Dean's office," Mr. Pedersen says, and I swear he's holding back an eye roll. "I'm sending you to tell the Dean about this mess and to get her to contact the police."

There's a collective intake of breath.

"The police?" Marie asks. Her gaze lands quickly on the dead cat before going back to the teacher, where it has been firmly planted since the beginning of this whole debacle. "For a dead cat?"

"Yes, Marie," Mr. Pedersen replies. "The police." I swear, it's the first time I've heard him getting annoyed with her. It's kind of refreshing.

"Off you go, Robert." Mr. Pedersen makes a shooing motion. "All the boys, out. Tell the Dean, then ask her to figure out where to put you until we get this mess straightened out."

They all grumble but follow orders. I hear someone giving Daniel a hard time for throwing up in the hallway, but less than a minute later, they're out of the building.

Mr. Pedersen crosses to the spot where Robert stood earlier. A frown appears as he sees the head on the floor, but he draws a deep breath, places his hands on his hips and glares at all of us.

"All right," he says. "Who did this?"

I freeze. He thinks one of us did it? Why not the boys?

He must have read my thought on my face. "The boys didn't do it. Their acting isn't good enough to pull off a genuine reaction like that." He glances at the bloody desk. "And they'd have done it outside, in hiding somewhere. This…this was set up by someone with a theatrical streak the size of the Antarctic."

My eyes automatically go to Marie. To my surprise, she's already looking at me.

"The only place I've seen a cleaver like that," she says, "is at Elisabeth's house. Norwegians don't use knives that big."

But my Chinese mother does. I gape at her. She's blaming this on me? Well, I guess I know who did it, then. Case closed.

But everybody's looking at me now, Mr. Pedersen included.

"I didn't—" I sputter to a stop. "I wouldn't—"

"The guillotine is French," Marie says.

And my dad's French. So, of course, I'd build a guillotine to kill a cat in my classroom. Makes perfect sense.

I point at the dead cat and finally find my voice. "I did not kill that cat."

"Nobody said you did," Mr. Pedersen says. But he's still looking at me, studying my reactions. Jesus, he actually thinks I could be the culprit?

"We all know what a guillotine is," I say. "We learned about it last week."

"I know," Mr. Pedersen says.

Ah. That's why he sent the boys away, free of all suspicion. In our class, all the girls take French, and the boys take German. We're real original like that.

I've been too focused on the teacher, so I haven't realized that the other girls have moved. Suddenly, I'm standing alone in front of the bloody mess on the front desks because the other girls have flocked around Marie in front of the blackboard.

She's got her biggest admirers flanking her; Charlotte and Christine on one side, and Nina on the other. Erin and Guro stand just an extra step back—they know they still haven't passed muster to be in the inner circle. I want to sneer at them for selling out, but I have bigger fish to fry at the moment.

I feel like I'm in court, with Mr. Pedersen as the judge and

Marie and her clique as the jury—who will probably need all of five seconds to declare me guilty.

I need to regroup. Look at this objectively.

I know I didn't kill that poor cat. I'm going to assume Mr. Pedersen didn't, either. He's clearly working on the assumption that one of the girls from the class did the deed—and I'm tempted to agree. Why would someone external to the class go through the trouble of setting everything up inside a locked classroom?

"The door was locked," I say to Mr. Pedersen. "None of us have the key."

Mr. Pedersen's gaze is inscrutable as silence settles.

"You did last week," he finally says, his voice soft.

I did. We all did, at some point. We'd been working in the gymnasium all day to set up for the school play, and several of us had borrowed the key from the teacher at one point or another to make a quick jaunt to the classroom to pick something up, or to bring something back.

"But you got the key back." I hate the little whine that makes its way into my voice.

"Doesn't take long to make a copy."

I wouldn't even know how to go about that, and I say as much.

Mr. Pedersen just shrugs.

"I'm not the only one who had the opportunity to make a copy," I say and point to the group of girls around Marie. "They did, too."

"I know," Mr. Pedersen says.

I hate whining and tattling, but I have to prove my innocence.

"It's a set-up," I whisper.

"What was that?" Mr. Pedersen asks. "Speak up, Elisabeth."

"They set me up," I say, my voice stronger.

"Who did?"

I point at the girls, my finger shaking, damn it. "Them. They've been after me for months, and I don't even know why."

I clear my throat and try to soldier on, but I've actually lost my train of thought.

I used to be friends with Marie and the rest of them. Then one day, I was out in the cold. No explanation, no angry words. Just silence, upturned noses, and deliberate slights throughout the day. At first, I'd tagged along, assuming everything would go back to normal.

An afternoon of insults yelled across the schoolyard for everyone to hear put a stop to that. I became a loner instead.

I've gotten used to their little games, but this is taking things too far. I'm just glad I don't have a cat, or I'm sure it would have been my animal lying there in a puddle of blood.

"Whose cat is that, anyway?" I ask. There are stray cats in the neighborhood, but the fur that's not covered in blood seems well-groomed, and I'd say it's well fed. Was.

All eyes go to the poor beast.

"Wait..." Charlotte takes a step forward, her perfectly plucked eyebrows drawn together. "Is that...?" She steps around the teacher's desk to get a look at the head.

"Kevin!" Her scream makes me jump back a step.

She's named her cat Kevin?

"You killed Charlotte's cat?" Marie moves to put her arms

around her friend and pats her head as she sobs into her shoulder. "How could you?"

"I didn't kill her cat!" I'm screaming even louder than Charlotte, as if the one screaming the loudest will be believed.

Charlotte pulls a tear-and-mascara streaked face from Marie's shoulder long enough to add her two cents. "What did Kevin ever do to you? It's no wonder you have no friends. You're a freak and a monster!"

"That's enough." Mr. Pedersen's calm and adult voice makes us all take a collective deep breath. "Charlotte," he says and puts a hand on her shoulder. "Why don't you and Christine go and wait in the hallway? I'll make sure you can bring Kevin home for a proper funeral once we're done here, all right?"

Hiccupping with every step, Charlotte follows Mr. Pedersen's suggestion. Christine doesn't seem too happy with leaving her queen behind, but Marie gives a regal nod, and the two girls close the door behind them.

Erin and Guro are holding hands, their fingers clutching each other so tightly their knuckles are white. Erin's gaze is fixed on the dead cat and I'd say she's well on her way into shock. She looked much the same when she'd caught her own foot on a fishing hook last summer and had to go to the ER to get it removed.

Guro stares daggers at me. We used to be friends. I'm floored to realize she believes Marie's story over mine. She actually thinks I'm capable of killing a cat—with a bloody guillotine!—just to…I don't even know what my motive is supposed to be, honestly.

"She did this to get back at us for standing up against her," Marie says to Mr. Pedersen.

Oh, for crying out… Fine, that could make some sense, if someone believes her entire narrative.

"You're not the one standing up to me," I say as tears threaten to fall. "I'm the one who's all alone because you decided to freeze me out."

One tear escapes and makes a straight line for my jaw.

I'm so pissed right now. Not only have they made my life miserable over the last few months, but on top of that, they're forcing me to show how much it has hurt? *And* I need to convince Mr. Pedersen that I'm not a cat-killer.

I decide to face off against him instead. I'm never going to win against Marie, but at least I can make sure my teacher believes me.

"I've been completely excluded from everything since October," I say. "Yes, that makes me angry—"

"I know," Mr. Pedersen says.

"You know…?"

"I know you've not been hanging out with the other girls for a while, Elisabeth."

He knew? He knew I'd been miserable and did nothing?

I'd actually played with the idea of talking to him about my troubles. It's what they tell you to do—if you're being bullied, go to the teachers and they'll help. I hadn't been convinced by this, and it turns out my doubts had been well founded.

He knew and had just let Marie do her thing.

I feel myself deflate. My shoulders hunch and my arms cross over my chest. A year and a half before high school. Might as well be a hundred.

"What I don't know," Mr. Pedersen says, "is whether that was your choice or theirs."

"It was definitely hers, Mr. Pedersen," Marie says, her voice earnest.

God, I hate her fake ass.

She isn't done. "I sincerely hope that the murderer will be severely punished. Charlotte loved that cat like a sibling."

"Rest assured," Mr. Pedersen says with a sigh. "The culprit will be punished. But we need to figure out who did it first."

"It was her!" Marie raises her voice for the first time and points her manicured finger at me. "There can be no doubt about it, Mr. Pedersen. She killed the cat to get back at me and my friends."

"Get back for what?" Mr. Pedersen's voice is silky smooth.

I hold my breath.

"I don't know!" Marie wails. "I don't know why she hates us, I just know that she does."

Damn her for being so convincing. And for using my arguments, which would make me look like a copycat. If she can fake the feeling this easily, it means she understands perfectly what she's making me go through. Somehow, that makes everything ten times worse.

My eyes fall to the scene of the crime in front of me. I just can't look at Marie anymore, and I don't want to risk seeing accusation in Mr. Pedersen's eyes.

The guillotine looks so morbid. It had sounded weird and exciting when we'd talked about it in French class, but here, with the blade gleaming and the blood glistening, it's just gruesome.

Thank God we have no death penalty in Norway, nor in France for that matter.

The wooden crate is a little out of place. It looks like one of those boxes my parents sometimes use to store jars of jam and pickled fruits. In fact…

I step closer and lean in to study the lower corner of the crate.

"What are you doing?" Marie says. "Mr. Pedersen, she's trying to tamper with the evidence."

I ignore her. I'm not planning on touching anything.

"The crate says Thorholm Fishing," I say.

I'm met with silence, so I look up. Mr. Pedersen is frowning at the crate. Marie is frowning at Mr. Pedersen. Nina has her eyes on her queen, waiting for orders—do these girls seriously have no self-respect?—and Guro and Erin are still trying to maim each other's hands. The two wannabe subjects exchange glances and I get a queasy feeling in my stomach.

I've seen this logo before. In fact, I've seen crates like these before.

"I must be getting old," Mr. Pedersen says, his eyes still on the crate. "My memory is failing me. Tell me, Erin, where does your father work again?"

Erin's basement. That's where I've seen the crates. Her father owns the factory down on the docks and brings home the crates so his wife can fill the garage with homemade jam.

"I didn't…" Erin's voice is close to a squeak.

"Is that crate from your home, Erin?" Mr. Pedersen asks.

She doesn't speak, but the tears streaking down her face are answer enough. She's still holding Guro's hand and her friend has started crying, too.

I try to picture Erin setting up the guillotine. Getting the cat. Convincing the cat to stay still while she lets the blade fall?

"You didn't do it alone," I say. "You'd need to be at least two to hold the animal in place or there's no way you'd get such a clean kill."

"Oh my God," Marie suddenly says. "I can't believe you killed Charlotte's cat! We invite you to be friends with us and this is how you repay us?"

I'm having trouble keeping up. I'm still stuck on my old friends becoming cat killers. And now Marie has turned her back on me for the first time since she accused me of being behind the cat murder and is laying into her so-called friends.

For Erin, it's the last straw. She goes from silently crying to outright bawling. I don't understand what she's trying to say, but I think "sorry" is every third word or so, and she even says my name.

What did I have to do with anything? I didn't do it, it's not my cat, I'm not the one to get decapitated.

I glance back to Mr. Pedersen. He's the teacher, the adult, shouldn't he be doing something?

His eyes are on Marie while she has her back turned. His expression is so far from his usually easygoing manner that I'm wondering if it's still the same guy. His face is drawn into hard lines and I can see the muscles of his jaw working—he must be grinding his teeth together. His eyes are laser sharp and I think his breathing is quicker than usual.

But he doesn't say anything.

Marie continues her show, with Nina as first violin. "Seriously," she says, "you think you know someone and then, bam! They go and kill your god-damned cat. What did Kevin ever do to you? I hope they expel you for this, I really do. I hope I'll never have to see your ugly mugs ever again."

Erin is still inconsolable and incomprehensible, but Guro finally speaks up. "But you told us to—"

"Oh, oh, oh!" Marie is screaming now. "I told you to what? Are you seriously going to blame this on me? What were you going to say? That I'd told you to kidnap Kevin and have him executed in our classroom? Seriously? You think anyone's going to buy that?

"If I told you to murder the Dean, would you do *that*? You do have minds of your own, don't you? You can't think for yourselves? Seriously, you expect me to *think* for you? You have to do *some* things for yourselves."

"But...but..." Guro doesn't get any further before she collapses into the arms of Erin and the two of them sink to the floor in a heap of arms, hair, tears, and hiccups.

"All right, Marie," Mr. Pedersen says. "That's enough."

"Mr. Pedersen." Marie manages a look so haughty I'm actually reminded of a painting of Marie Antoinette we'd studied in French class. "I hope they will be adequately punished for their crime."

"Marie, enough." His voice is calm, but even Marie catches the undercurrent of anger.

She shuts up.

"Marie, Nina, why don't you go join your friends in the hallway and bring them with you to the Dean's office. Tell the Dean I need her to occupy the class at least until lunch."

With a regal nod, Marie grabs Nina by the elbow and exits the room.

Why didn't he send me out, too?

I look to Mr. Pedersen for clues, but his focus is on the heap of crying teenagers on the floor. He still looks hard and angry, but his stance has turned into something more reluctant.

I take a tentative step toward the door. "Can I…?"

"Guess you're off the hook this time," he says.

"Who, me?"

"Yes, you." He sighs and nods his head toward Erin and Guro. "Those two aren't, so…"

I just stare at him.

"You do realize this was just her backup plan?" His gaze lands on the dead cat, but I'm not sure he's actually seeing it. "You were her primary target, but if she couldn't make it stick, those two would just have to do."

God, it makes so much sense.

What have I ever done to deserve such hate? She'd kill her best friend's cat to get me? To get pretty much *anyone*? Would she have thrown Nina or Charlotte to the wolves, too, if she had the chance?

"You have to stop her," I tell my teacher. "Please tell me she'll get expelled for this. Or at least suspended."

Mr. Pedersen hangs his head. "She didn't actually do anything."

"Yes, she did!"

He waves a hand to indicate the girls crying on the floor. "These two will confess as soon as they're coherent. I'm sure they'll tell us how Marie manipulated them, but I'm equally sure Marie and the rest of her clique will deny it." He runs both hands through his hair and pulls it in frustration. "And she's right, dammit. Why couldn't they think for themselves? They were the ones to actually do the deed."

My mouth is working, but no sound is coming out.

"Go join the rest of the class in the administrative building, will you?" Even though he's talking to me, his eyes are on Erin and Guro. "And stay away from Marie."

ଔ

THE COOL BOYS are still shoving at each other and the uncool boys are still hunched over their phones. The cool girls are still gossiping and I'm still on high alert.

The seat at the back of the class is still mine, and I'm still counting dust motes.

But we're not drawing sixty-degree angles anymore. Mr. Pedersen doesn't lean over Marie's desk to show her things when she asks questions. He stays at the blackboard.

The two seats in front of mine, where Erin and Guro used to sit, are empty.

And Charlotte has changed seats, from the one next to Marie to the one on my left. So far, we've only exchanged hellos, but I'm confident we'll get there.

One down, the rest of the class to go.

We'll get there.

THE ART OF PRETENDING

I'm an expert at being the New Guy — a side effect of parents who move you to a different city every couple of years. A bonus? I can decide how to portray myself to new classmates and future friends.

For our most recent move, I decided to go with Funny Guy, but it takes more work than anticipated, especially since I'm a fade-into-the-wallpaper natural.

While giving Funny Guy my best go at a party, things get… weird.

And I discover I'm not the only New Guy in town after all.

Being the new kid in school is never easy. You need to pick a tactic for fitting in—whatever that might mean for you—and stick with it. If you start off super confident, only to turn into a shy little mouse the minute someone talks back to you, you're doomed. If you go for the easy solution of hanging with the quiet kids and then turn out to be too loud for them, you're burning all kinds of bridges.

You have to know yourself, and you have to know where you want to be.

For those who never change schools, they don't have to turn all introspective and wonder *who they are*, *really*, before they show up to class. They're doing the same thing they've always done, with minor variations as they try on new possibilities, but they never stray far. Those who make big alterations *believe* they've changed, but don't realize that their classmates see the change for the disguise it is. They've known you long enough to know what lies underneath.

But when you're new? Well, it's scary, sure. All alone in a body of people who've known each other since they were six. Everybody stares at you, whispers to their friends whatever first impression they have of you. But it's also freeing.

You can do—and be—*whatever* you want.

This time, I know we're only staying for a couple of months, so I want to try something new and scary. The window is too short to make any real friends so I might as well make it interesting.

I want to be the loud and funny dude. I've always wondered what that was like.

That is *so* not me. Don't get me wrong, I have a sense of humor. But it's best expressed in cynical remarks and sarcastic comebacks. The kind of humor that will make only a few people laugh—but that's okay, because they're the best ones.

But the funny dude? He has to make everyone laugh. Someone attacks you? Make fun of them in a way that will make the rest of the student body roar with laughter, and the bully will leave you be. A teacher humiliates you? Crack a joke at your own expense, making it seem like you *want* everybody to laugh at you. If they laugh, you're the winner, not the loser. You want to impress a guy? Make him laugh, preferably at something that makes you come off as cute, or smart, or, well, funny.

Like I said, it's not really me. But these guys have fascinated me for a while now. What motivates them to make themselves targets like that? How do they come up with jokes in any and all situations? Are there self help books to learn how to be the right kind of funny? Is it really possible to smile and crack jokes at all hours of the day?

So I've decided I'll make an experiment of it. Two months of being the funny dude should help me answer several of my questions.

Of course, if I can't manage to keep up the charade, my two months in this place will be torture. A funny dude who isn't funny? He doesn't survive long in high school.

I'm fairly certain I'm funny enough and smart enough come up with the jokes. The biggest challenge is going to be being loud enough. Drawing attention is counter-intuitive, if you ask me. But I'll try anything once.

So far, two weeks in, it's going pretty well. I think. I wish I had at least one friend who could listen in on other people's conversations to figure out what they think of me. Because the first thing I've discovered? When you crack jokes at everyone and everything, it's impossible to have a serious conversation. You'll learn real quick who can take a joke and who will hide in the bathroom for the rest of recess, who will fire back with their own brand of humor, landing solid hits even without knowing anything about you, and who sees you as an excellent side-dish at any party, standing at the ready to throw jokes into any awkward silence.

That's how it feels, anyway.

This guy Thomas invited me to his party tonight. His parents are out of town for the weekend and they apparently trust him enough to leave him here alone. I don't think I'm taking much of a risk by saying they will regret their decision when they get back on Sunday.

Someone emptied a bag of extra-salty chips in the couch earlier but nobody can be bothered to clean it up, so they're just sitting in it, making sure the grease is well and truly smeared into the cushions. One girl insisted on drinking her wine out of a wine glass but was too short to reach them and proceeded to break at least half the family's glassware when she climbed up on the kitchen counter to reach them.

And that's just the stuff I've seen from here.

Here being the most central spot I could find. I'm seated on the armrest of the couch, with a view of the entire living room and most of the kitchen. If I lean forward, I can see the bathroom door down the hall.

If I'm going to be making jokes all night long, I need as much inspiration fodder as I can get.

I feel like I'm doing pretty well so far. The group of guys who have been occupying the couch for the last half-hour are including me in their banter and seem to expect me to make them laugh at least every two or three minutes. Whenever one of them says something, they pause for a second to let me interrupt with a joke if I have one. So far, I've managed to follow up on at least two thirds. Not all the jokes were funny, but then this group has downed half a bottle of vodka already between them and would probably find the phone book funny if read in the right tone.

Still, I feel like I've been made part of the group, which is nice. Usually, when I'm just plain old me, it takes me way longer than two weeks to integrate a friend group. Even though it's exhausting, there might be something to this funny dude business.

But right now, I need a break. Just a short one, to let my facial muscles relax and my mind zone out for a bit. People who do stand up comedy for a living must be superhuman.

I tell the guys I'm going to take a leak and step into the hallway. But instead of going into the bathroom on my left, I turn right and walk straight into whichever room this might be. I don't care what it is as long as it's empty.

It isn't.

And no, before you get any ideas, it's not *that*. From what I've understood, those activities are taken upstairs, where there are three bedrooms to choose from but none of them have locks. I quickly decided I'd stay downstairs. I do *not* care if girls find funny dudes attractive. And so far I haven't picked up on anybody batting for my team.

Anyway, back to the not-empty room.

I think maybe it's a game room. Or an office. Or a gym. Or maybe a library. It's a room that does multitasking really well. And honestly, the furniture and things scattered around the space become kind of insignificant when there are two Thomases staring at each other across a foosball table in the corner.

This might explain why he hasn't been present at his own party, letting an increasingly drunk group of teenagers run free in his parents' house.

"I'm telling you, you're not ready!" the Thomas on the left yells. "You're still way too obvious." I guess he was yelling before I came in, that's why neither of them has noticed me yet.

"Not obvious," the Thomas on the right says. "Like you exactly."

There's something weird about his voice. It's the same as the first Thomas, except it's not. Something's missing. Depth. It's kinda like talking to someone on the phone. You recognize the voice but it's missing frequencies or something.

Left-Thomas slams a hand into the foosball table, making it rattle. "You might have figured out the body, but the minute you open your mouth, they're going to figure out what you are."

Okay, what am I missing? I hate feeling stupid. I did notice something odd the minute Right-Thomas opened his mouth, but I don't know what he is. It's supposed to be obvious? I compared his voice to a phone, so…he's a robot?

"Nobody believe," Right-Thomas says with the certainty of a five-year-old. If he says that's how it is, then that's how it is. "You say so. Aliens not exist."

Alien.

Sure. Yeah.

I'll have to agree with Right-Thomas. Aliens don't exist.

He might be a robot, though. A badly programmed one who can't create complete sentences.

Left-Thomas throws up his arms. "Well, they'll start believing once they realize you're not me and morph into a table because it has a pretty color!"

Huh.

Without moving anything but my eyes, I try to scan the room for hidden cameras. Could this be some sort of set-up to pull a prank on the new kid? On the funny dude who isn't all that funny? I don't see anything suspicious, although I suppose the camera on the laptop in the corner might be on and recording even though the screen is dark. But nobody told me to come in here.

"Cobalt blue very pretty," Right-Thomas says. There's no defensiveness in his voice, only firm confirmation, a statement of fact.

He flickers blue—cobalt blue.

And not just his skin. It's the whole package, jeans, hair, tight t-shirt, and white sneakers included. A flash of blue, then he's back to normal Thomas-colors. He cocks an eyebrow at Left-Thomas as if he has proved his point.

All right, I think it's time to rename them Real-Thomas and…Alien-Thomas?

Really?

Could those guys from earlier have slipped something into my drink while I wasn't watching? Some hallucinatory drug? Shouldn't I have felt that? Oh, who am I kidding, I have no idea what it feels like to take drugs.

But I could have sworn this isn't it.

Real-Thomas waves at Alien-Thomas's body. "See? This is what I'm talking about! Humans don't go changing colors because they thought of something pretty. You've never managed to keep the shape for more than five minutes. There's no way you're surviving an entire party!"

Alien-Thomas folds his arms and lifts his chin in a movement I realize he has perfectly copied from Real-Thomas. He does that when he's having an argument with someone during recess and won't budge no matter what anyone throws at him.

It's kind of awesome.

"This why alcohol," Alien-Thomas says in his slightly off-tune voice. "They all drunk. Not recognize who me, who you."

Real-Thomas buries his face in his hands and lets out a groan. "Even dead drunk, if they don't realize when I've been switched out with an alien, it means I need new friends."

I laugh.

Two identical heads whip around to stare at me.

I flash a smile. When in doubt, always smile. "Sorry to interrupt," I say lamely. "But that was funny. And you might be right about needing new friends—your current ones are trashing your house."

I don't think Real-Thomas heard a word I said. He's frozen in place, his mouth hanging open as he stares uncomprehendingly at me with his pretty brown eyes. You'd think I was the one talking to an alien copy of myself.

Alien-Thomas is eying the door with a speculative look. I take a step to the right to block the exit, just in case. I don't think the people out there are drunk enough—yet—to not realize there's something wrong with this Thomas.

In fact... I take two steps toward the foosball table, leaning in to get the light from the ceiling to hit at a different angle on his skin. "You don't look so good, dude." His skin is as smooth and soft-looking as Thomas's, sure, but it has a sickly cast.

Real-Thomas comes out of his funk on a great sigh. "He can't see the colors on the red side of the spectrum, so he can't copy them." He waves a hand at his copy. "This is what I'd look like with no red blood running through my veins."

I break into a huge smile. "You're telling me he has blue

blood? Like royalty?"

I gotta admit, I'm proud to have thought of that so quickly. And the happy feeling increases when Real-Thomas snorts a laugh.

Silence falls. Real-Thomas is watching his feet. Alien-Thomas is studying me and I don't like being under this level of scrutiny.

"He's not going to copy me next, is he?"

Real-Thomas's eyes lift to meet mine and a wistful smile plays across his lips. "Don't worry, he needs to spend a lot more time with you to manage that. And study you much more closely."

My eyes narrow. "How close, exactly?"

Real-Thomas's laughter seems to surprise him as much as it does me. "I think it might be best I keep that a trade secret."

I realize too late I'm just standing there, smiling goofily. Way to make a good impression. "So, uh…" Nope, I have no idea what I'm going to say. "Alien?" I finish lamely.

Real-Thomas looks at his copy and sighs. "According to my dad's definition, yes. He's from outer space and is sentient." He pulls himself a little higher and I can see the joke on his face before he gives it voice. "I guess, technically, he's a martian."

Alien-Thomas seems happy not to participate in our conversation. Arms crossed, his eyes never leave me. I hope Real-Thomas is right and this won't be enough for him to copy me. I'm great and all, but one of me is more than enough.

I focus on Thomas. "Are you telling me he's from Mars? How do you know? Can you trust what he tells you?"

Thomas winces. "I may have…uh…stolen him from my dad's office?"

"And your dad's office is...on Mars?"

Thomas bursts out laughing. It's a full-belly laugh and he throws his head back so I can see his perfect teeth all the way back to the molars. "Yeah, sure," he says once the laughter quiets down. "That's why I was away from school for a week at the end of last year. I was on Mars, stealing aliens from my dad's office."

Staying perfectly serious, I shrug. "I wouldn't know. I didn't live here last year."

"Right. You're only here for a couple of months, from what I hear?"

It's the first time anyone here is paying me any kind of attention and I'm thrilled. Really. Especially when it comes from someone like Thomas. But... "I'd love to tell you all about it, dude, but maybe first we address the alien in the room?"

Thomas deflates a little and he shoves his hands into this jeans' pockets. "Right. Well, my dad doesn't have an office on Mars. But he does work at the CNES, you know the space research center? Sorry, of course you know. Who doesn't? Anyway, he worked on the mission that sent a robot to Mars, and is in charge of studying all the stuff the robot brought back."

I dart a quick glance at Alien-Thomas—he's still staring at my face with a scrutiny I don't like. "Are you telling me you stole an *alien*? And he didn't notice? He didn't notice, right? He wouldn't actually let you steal an actual alien and play with it in your home."

His expression answers my questions. No, the dad doesn't know.

"He didn't realize it was an alien," Thomas mumbles. "And neither did I, at first. As you can see"—He waves a hand at his almost-perfect copy.—"he's really good at imitating things around him. He'd been imitating a rock for…I still don't know how long. He doesn't really understand the concept of time."

I exhale and let it sink in. I'm in a room with a real-life *alien*.

Despite the unnerving stare from Alien-Thomas, I turn to face him, to really study him.

He's flawless. A part from the lack of red, of course. But if I hadn't known Thomas, I would just have taken him for someone who never saw the sun. The voice was weird, but only because I was comparing it to the original. If I hadn't known Thomas, I wouldn't have picked up on anything.

I try for my sternest expression as I stare into Alien-Thomas's brown eyes. "How many of you are there on Earth right now, parading around and pretending to be human?"

His expression doesn't change at *all*.

"He's still working on facial expressions," Thomas says. He has stepped closer so we're standing shoulder to shoulder, facing off against Alien-Thomas. "He can do smiles, frowns, lifted eyebrows, but he doesn't understand the intricacies of the emotions involved, so it's kinda hard to know when to do what. I've been trying to read Dad's books on artificial intelligence, to try to understand how people explain emotions to machines, but, well, it's well above my grade level, honestly."

"How do you know you can trust him?" I ask. "How can we be sure they're not taking over the Earth, copy by copy? How do you even know it's a 'he?'"

Thomas shrugs and his shoulder brushes against mine. "I don't. But first he copied my dog and now me, so I'm going with he." He chews on his lip for a moment. "I don't think they have sexes, honestly. And to answer your first question, no, I don't think there are aliens running around all over our planet. I think he has emotions. To a certain degree, anyway. He's definitely curious. He sees something new, something he doesn't understand, and he wants to copy it. But I've never witnessed anything to indicate he wants to take over the world, or even the house. He just wants to learn."

"So what happens if he *can't* learn?" Is that when the alien invasion will begin? When he's learned everything he can from us and moves on to bigger fish?

Us? Seems I'm not planning on turning Thomas in to the authorities.

Thomas shrugs. "He spent centuries as a rock on Mars. I don't think we have to worry about his patience running out in our lifetime."

I've been staring at Alien-Thomas since the beginning of this conversation. He hasn't blinked once. It's making me nervous. And he's going to have to work on that if he wants to pass for human outside of this room.

Yep, I've definitely included myself in the team.

Alien-Thomas's face flickers. His eyes change from brown to green. His nose narrows and lengthens. One of his front teeth becomes crooked.

"Hey! No copying me!" I give him a shove in the chest. "Stop it! Keep Thomas's face, dude." I look down at my hand, feeling like it has tricked me, somehow. Where I expected to feel soft cloth with warm body underneath, I felt only cold stone.

"Oh, yeah, he also can't change his temperature," Thomas says. "He's always room temperature. And solid as a rock, no matter what he looks like. Which is why"—he's leaning forward, making sure Alien-Thomas's eyes meet his—"he will *never* be able to pass for human and we have to be very, very careful. You do *not* want to end up locked up somewhere so scientists can study you to death."

I reach out to touch Alien-Thomas's arm. Hard rock. Fascinating.

"Why do you want to pass for human so bad, anyway?" I ask Alien-Thomas. "If you can change into anything, surely, it would be less conspicuous if you become, like, a cat, or something?"

He's back to wearing Thomas's face, thank god. "Like communicate. Learn talk. Already be dog. Human complex."

We should definitely worry about what happens when he's learned everything. I turn my back to Alien-Thomas and pull on Thomas so he does the same. "Humans are just about the most complicated thing that exists on earth," I whisper. "What happens when he knows everything?"

Thomas doesn't seem worried. "You think he'll learn everything there is to know about humans in a week? It took him *two months* to imitate the dog well enough for us to attempt a couple of exits where people could see him. Copying my body has taken him five months—and it's not even perfect. I don't think he'll ever get the voice right. Can't hear all the frequencies."

"Even if it takes years," I insist. "This is your typical beginning of a SciFi horror movie. He learns everything, brings in his buddies, and they take over the world."

Brown eyes crinkle and my heart does a somersault. "We must not have watched the same movies," he says. "Besides, I've been unable to ascertain he has buddies. He doesn't have a very good grasp of time, but I think he's been on Mars as a rock for longer than humanity has been walking the Earth."

"Are *all* the rocks on Mars aliens?"

Thomas shrugs. "How would I know? I don't think any of the others the robot brought back were. They would have changed into something other than rock by now, and we'd have heard about it."

"But when he learns everything—"

"Dude, you've got to stop worrying about that." Thomas puts a hand on my arm and I'm suddenly hyper-aware of his body next to mine. Nice and warm, and not at all stone-like. "How is he supposed to learn *everything* about humans? *We* don't know everything. And that's just if we're talking about facts and science and stuff. He's having trouble with basics like why the same thing will make me happy and my sister miserable. Any emotion other than curiosity is way out of his league right now. Now do something more complicated, like trying to flirt with a girl. If *we're* having trouble with it, imagine what a basket case he will be. You get him to set flirting as a goal and he should be occupied for years."

"Talk for yourself," I grumble and ease away so we're no longer touching. "I have no interest in flirting with *girls*." Uh-oh, I didn't intend to accentuate the last word like that.

"Huh." The look Thomas is giving me is eerily similar to the one Alien-Thomas was giving me earlier.

When he doesn't appear to have anything else to add, I figure it's best to change the subject. "What does he eat? Don't your parents notice if they're feeding an extra person?"

Thomas blinks. Glances over his shoulder at his alien copy. "He runs on solar energy."

"Say what now?"

"He needs solar energy to function. If he doesn't get his daily dose, he gets all sluggish. If it's cloudy, he needs to stay out there for *hours* before he's full."

"He spends *hours* in your garden and your parents haven't noticed?" I'm starting to worry they're of the neglecting sort, which isn't great news for Thomas.

"You forget he knows how to look like a rock." Before I can wrap my mind around this information, he does a one-eighty on our conversation. "You're really not interested in girls? How do you know?"

"Uh…" I hadn't planned on coming out in this school. It's just so much work and bother, I usually stay quiet when our stay is short. But I guess that ship has sailed. And if I'm not mistaken, Thomas has shifted closer. I can smell his cheap cologne. It may be in my best interest to answer his question.

"I just know. I have no wish to get close to any girls, don't feel like touching or kissing them. They're nice to hang out with and talk to, but that's it. Now, boys…" I sigh happily. "Them I can imagine doing things with."

"Imagine?"

My heart is beating a million times a minute. I'm acutely aware of my arm touching Thomas's and of his beautiful eyes focused on my face. I'm not sure if I'm still breathing as all my energy goes into not letting my internal scream become external. Is he flirting? Are we flirting? How do I know?

And yeah, Thomas is totally right. There's no way we can explain this with words and logic to Alien-Thomas so he'll know how to behave if someone is flirting with him.

He's still just standing there, by the way. Not at all bothered by us turning our backs on him to discuss him like he's not there. Any normal person would have said something, left the room, started doing something else… The alien just stands there, his eyes on the back of my head, studying every detail.

I'll have to worry about that later.

"I haven't had the opportunity for practical work yet. Are you offering?" I've stopped breathing. Maybe I could pretend it was a joke if he turns me down? Except I'm pretty sure my face gives me away.

"Can I practice?" Alien-Thomas asks.

"No!" Thomas and I yell in unison. We whip around, both of us holding our hands out as if to ward him off.

"I don't care how much you look like Thomas," I say before I can think things through. "I'm not kissing a rock." I run the words through my mind. "Uh."

Thomas points at his alien copy. "No practicing kissing." Turns back to me, a huge smile on his face. "I'm one of the boys you can imagine doing things with?"

Okay, this could end badly. I read a boy's reaction wrong a year ago and earned a black eye for my efforts.

But that grin isn't a mocking one. Far from it.

It's the grin of a guy who's happy to be wanted.

"I, uh…" Words aren't making sense anymore. I'm smiling back, though. I don't think I could stop if I wanted to. Still, words would be good right about now.

"You practice," Alien-Thomas says. "I watch." He steps closer, no more than an inch from my shoulder, and focuses on my lips.

"No!" We agree again.

"Okay." Thomas grabs his copy by the elbow and pulls him toward the door. "You're going to my room. And no coming out until everybody's gone! You can try copying the light again. I'm sure you can figure it out if you study it closely enough."

He rips open the door—

"Thomas! There you are! You have to taste this drink. Vodka and Fanta is, like, the most fantastic thing *ever*!"

Uh oh. Alien-Thomas is visible to the drunk idiots in the hallway, as am I two steps behind him. But Thomas, the real one, is still hidden behind the open door.

Our eyes meet. Now what?

Alien-Thomas reacts before we can. "I taste Fanta. Fizz! I taste fantastic thing ever!" And he steps into the hallway.

The door slowly slides shut. We're left in complete silence.

"How drunk were those guys?" Thomas whispers.

"Pretty drunk." I try for an optimistic expression. "They didn't notice he speaks weird. They'll probably think *he's* drunk."

"And if they touch him?" His hand goes to his forehead.

I grab his hand before panic can set in and pull it down between us. "They're pretty drunk. Too drunk to conclude he's an alien who looks exactly like you. It's like a real-life test where you'll be allowed to delete the record if it's a fail."

Thomas tears free and goes for the door. "I have to go save him."

I jump after him, slamming him into the door. "If you go out there, they *will* know something's up. Let him…uh…" I've noticed how close we're standing. I'm basically flattened against him. I feel his heat from knees to head. His cologne somehow smells pleasing just because it's his.

His cheeks weren't this red earlier, I'm sure of it. Not that my cheeks must be much better.

"Let him what?" Thomas asks. But I don't think he's asking about his alien.

"Do what he wants." I gulp. "Practice." My gaze drops to his lips.

Neither of us is breathing. I can hear a mosquito zooming somewhere behind me and a drunken roar comes through the door.

Then we're kissing. I don't know who started it. I don't care.

Yes. It's already perfect, but practice can't hurt, right?

I have no idea how long we stand there, practicing, completely ignoring the sounds of our classmates trashing the living room, but it's the best time of my life.

Until a *scream* makes both of us step back.

"What's happening?" Thomas reaches for the door knob.

"Hey." I place my hand on his. "Let me go out and look. No point in outing Alien-Thomas if someone saw a mouse."

"Alien-Thomas?"

I shrug, pull open the door, and slip out.

Chaos.

Everybody seems to be screaming—and heading for the door. The front door is open and one, two, three girls run out while I'm watching, wide-eyed. Clément, one of the guys I was entertaining earlier, hops past, trying to pull on his sneaker while running.

"What's going on?" I yell.

"Thomas turned into a stone!" Clément's voice is a good octave higher than usual. "He drank the vodka Fanta we made for him and just—*poof!*—turned into a friggin' *stone*! I'm outta here before the police show up!"

Fifteen seconds later, the house is empty.

Thomas emerges behind me. "Everybody's gone?"

I nod as I walk over to stop the music. Loud disco music when nobody's partying is just weird and sad. "I don't think vodka agreed with Alien-Thomas."

"Drink dangerous!" Alien-Thomas appears in the kitchen door. His expression is the same neutral he's worn since I met him, but I sense he's upset.

"Alcohol *is* dangerous," I agree. "You should probably stay away from it in the future." I look to Thomas. "They saw him turn into a rock."

"Oh." Thomas nods. Nods again. And again. "That's going to be hard to explain on Monday."

"Mhmm." I look at the mess we're standing in without really seeing it. "They *were* pretty drunk."

"Maybe something else will happen this weekend to distract them." Thomas sighs. "Like a world war, or a cure for cancer or something. Actually, the cancer thing probably isn't big enough."

Oh, wait. I know something that's *always* big in high school.

"I can come out, if you want? I'll post something on Insta tomorrow. I think it's best if they have some time to work themselves into a frenzy ahead of time. Monday morning won't do the trick."

"You— You can't just offer to out yourself like that!"

I shrug. And the idea is growing on me. "Why not? It won't be the first time I've come out. Nor the last with the way my dad can never stay in one city for more than a few months at a time. It'll work, I promise." I start pacing, kicking at empty beer cans and plastic cups to clear a path. "I'll need to come up with a good picture to use, though. Posing with a Pride flag is a bit boring, don't you think? Not to mention I don't have one, so that could be problematic. Maybe I should wear makeup? Except that's not really me, so that's weird, right? Oh! Or maybe—"

Thomas cuts me off with a kiss.

When we come up for air, he says, "Snap a picture now. Get the mess in the background. It'll prove I'm not a stone. If someone starts talking about the stone business, they'll deviate to the picture, and to our coming out. It'll totally work."

"*Our* coming-out? Are you sure? This isn't a decision to take lightly. You were talking about flirting with girls less than thirty minutes ago."

"And talking was everything I was ever going to do on the subject, believe me." He twists around to look at Alien-Thomas currently staring at a puddle of spilled beer while on all fours on the floor with a level of concentration I can only dream about. "We have to protect him."

Alien-Thomas's tongue darts out to taste the beer.

He turns into a stone.

"That's fascinating," I mumble. "He's amenable to be studied like he's studying everything else?"

Thomas nods and his eyes twinkle. He knows he's won. "I didn't know about the alcohol, but he has a couple of other triggers you're going to want to see. I'm telling you, he's *fascinating*."

I pull my phone out of my pocket and turn on the front-facing camera. "All right, let's do this." I hold up the phone and aim it so the trashed living room is clearly visible behind me. "I can still do this solo if you want."

Thomas steps up next to me and wraps his arm around my waist. "No way. Go for it." He leans in to give me a peck on the cheek.

I snap the picture.

So maybe I won't be the funny dude this time around.

I'll just be me.

AUTHOR'S NOTE

THANK YOU FOR staying with me for these short Young Adult stories. I hope you enjoyed them! Feel free to leave a review or tell a friend, so the book can make more friends.

If you want more short stories, I have two other collections out: *Deep Dark Secrets* and *A Thief in the Night.* They are both mystery collections aimed at an adult audience, but there's no reason you wouldn't enjoy them. They're not *that* adult.

There's also the *Ghost Detective* serieses, one with standalone short stories (you can pick up the first one for free through my newsletter), and one with a series of novels.

You can find a complete list of my books in the next pages.

R.W. Wallace
www.rwwallace.com

ABOUT THE AUTHOR

R.W. WALLACE WRITES in most genres, though she tends to end up in mystery more often than not. Dead bodies keep popping up all over the place whenever she sits down in front of her keyboard.

The stories mostly take place in Norway or France; the country she was born in and the one that has been her home for two decades. Don't ask her why she writes in English—she won't have a sensible answer for you.

Her Ghost Detective short story series appears in *Pulphouse Magazine*, starting in issue #9.

You can find all her books, long and short, all genres, on rwwallace.com.

Also by R.W. Wallace

Mystery

Ghost Detective Novels
Beyond the Grave
Unveiling the Past
Beneath the Surface

Ghost Detective Shorts
Just Desserts
Lost Friends
Family Bonds
Common Ground
Till Death
Family History
Heritage
Eternal Bond
New Beginnings
Severed Ties

The Tolosa Mystery Series
The Red Brick Haze
The Red Brick Cellars
The Red Brick Basilica

Short Story Collections
Deep Dark Secrets
A Thief in the Night

Short Stories
Cold Blue Eternity
Hidden Horrors

Critters
Gertrude and the Trojan Horse
First Impressions
Let Them Eat Cake
Out of Sight
Sitting Duck
Two's Company
Like Mother Like Daughter

TIME TRAVEL SECRETS (SHORT STORIES)

Moneyline Secrets
Family Secrets

ROMANCE

FRENCH OFFICE ROMANCE SERIES
Flirting in Plain Sight
Hiding in Plain Sight
Loving in Plain Sight

SHORT STORIES
Down the Memory Aisle

HOLIDAY SHORT STORIES

Morbier Impossible
A Second Chance
The Magic of Sharing
The Case of the Disappearing Gingerbread City
The Lucia Crown

YOUNG ADULT (SHORT STORIES)

Unexpected Consequences
The Art of Pretending
First Impressions

www.ingramcontent.com/pod-product-compliance
Lightning Source LLC
LaVergne TN
LVHW041709060526
838201LV00043B/641